A Foreign Field

A Foreign Field

Gillian Chan

KIDS CAN PRESS

Kids Can Press acknowledges the financial support of the Ontario Arts Council,
the Canada Council for the Arts and the Government of Canada, through the
BPIDP, for our publishing activity.

Published in Canada by
Kids Can Press Ltd.
29 Birch Avenue
Toronto, ON M4V 1E2

Published in the U.S. by
Kids Can Press Ltd.
2250 Military Road
Tonawanda, NY 14150

www.kidscanpress.com

Edited by Charis Wahl
Designed by Karen Powers
Printed and bound in Canada

The hardcover edition of this book is smyth sewn casebound.
The paperback edition of this book is limp sewn with a drawn-on cover.

CM 02 0 9 8 7 6 5 4 3 2 1
CM PA 02 0 9 8 7 6 5 4 3 2 1

National Library of Canada Cataloguing in Publication Data

Chan, Gillian
    A foreign field

ISBN 1-55337-349-9 (bound)   ISBN 1-5537-350-2 (pbk.)

I. Title.

PS8555.H39243A86 2002   jC813'.54   C2001-903107-6
PZ7.C3588Fo 2002

Kids Can Press is a *l♥rus*™ Entertainment company

This book is for all the "eagles," young and old.
May you find friendly skies in which to fly.

✫   ✫   ✫

Per Ardua ad Astra
Through Adversity to the Stars
— The motto of the Royal Air Force

ACKNOWLEDGMENTS

Many people helped me with the research for this book, generously sharing both their expertise and personal stories. Any factual errors were, of course, made by the author alone! In particular, I would like to thank the following people: the staff at the Canadian Warplane Heritage museum in Mount Hope, who generously allowed me to clamber around the inside of their Avro Anson — the plane on which Stephen trained; Jim Willis, who patiently answered my questions about flying; George Neale, whose vivid memories of his flight training at SFTS 16, Hagersville, proved invaluable in imagining what it must have been like for Stephen; and my husband, Henry, for all his support and for thinking of the title. I should also like to thank the Canada Council and the Ontario Arts Council for their support for the writing of this book.

Gillian Chan
November 1, 2001
Dundas, Ontario

ONE

"Colin?" Ellen's voice bounced through the house. "Colin!" Her voice was sharper now. She just knew that her brother had sneaked out when she'd gone into the kitchen to check that the potatoes weren't boiling over. She stamped her foot, then felt silly. Colin was probably halfway to the air base already, even though Dad had forbidden him to go there. As if that would have stopped Colin. He would just try not to get caught. He was crazy about planes and would spend all day lying outside the fence at the end of the runway, watching the student pilots practice.

"Laddie," their father had said, his Scottish accent thick, as it always was when he was trying to sound stern, "you're not to go there. There's a war on, and those young men are here to train for combat, not to provide amusement for starry-eyed schoolboys!"

Colin had hung his head and said, "Yes, Dad," in a meek voice, but Ellen had seen what her father hadn't — Colin's fingers firmly crossed behind his back.

Ellen sighed and flopped down on the bottom step. If she went after Colin, dinner would spoil, and if she took everything off the stove, she would have a lot to explain once her parents got home and found no dinner waiting. It just wasn't fair. She ran her fingers through her thick, curly hair. Dad's work hours were longer than ever, and since Stewart had been reported missing at Dieppe in August, her mother had thrown herself into every kind of war work imaginable. It was all very well that it took Mum's mind off Stewart, and that she wanted to do her bit; but Ellen was left to try to control Colin and to keep the house going, too. Her friends weren't expected to do half of what she had to do — Barb and Deanna never got to see her outside school anymore. Besides, Mum wasn't the only one worried about Stewart.

Ellen smiled slightly. There was a certain guilty pleasure in feeling sorry for yourself. "Nobody likes me. Everybody hates me. Think I'll go and eat worms!" She repeated the rhyme her father always sang to them when they were whining about their lot in life. Her smile got broader and she started to dance along the hallway, stomping her feet to the rhythm as she shouted the words. She spun round, her arms held wide. "NObody likes ME! EVERYbody hates ME! THINK I'll go and EAT WORMS." Ellen's whirling dance stopped abruptly as she collided with the front door swinging inward. She fell back on the floor, and found herself looking up at two pairs of legs.

One set was instantly recognizable: scabby and

bony, slightly chapped, protruding from knee-length britches, socks half mast. Colin. The little brat had deigned to come home. She was all set to let rip when she checked the other set of legs. Blue serge — that particular shade of blue that belonged only to the Air Force. Ellen clambered to her feet — Graham must have got an unexpected pass and hitchhiked down from Trenton to see the family. Her eyes blurred with tears, Ellen threw her arms around Graham, only to step back immediately. She should have had to reach up to hug him, but whoever was standing there was about her height and much thinner than her burly brother. A wash of embarrassment coursed through Ellen. She hardly dared look at the stranger and certainly couldn't bring herself to speak.

Standing in the doorway, his face as deep a crimson as hers, was a young man in an RAF uniform. In one hand, he held his cap; the other had a tight grip on Colin's upper arm. Stuttering, he pushed Colin forward. "Excuse me, miss, is this your brother?"

Ellen decided that if he was going to ignore the mortifying way she had thrown her arms around him, so would she. "Yes," she said, but her voice was puzzled. Why had this complete stranger brought Colin home? "Has he got into some sort of mischief?" Before the young man could answer, Ellen turned on Colin. "Dad's going to kill you. He'll have your guts for garters if you've been messing around again!"

Colin looked mutinous. "I didn't mean anything. I just wanted a closer look, that's all."

Ellen glared at Colin, but he refused to meet her eye and tried to shrug off the stranger's hand. Confident that Colin was not going to run now he was home, the stranger let go of his arm. Colin moved away and made a big show of rubbing it.

The young man spoke. "Look, it was something and nothing. No harm was done this time, but it could be dangerous."

Ellen sighed. This was all too much. She had no idea what had happened, and knew she wouldn't get a straight answer out of Colin. "Look, you'd better come in and explain. I haven't any tea, but I could offer you a lemonade. I made some this morning." Ellen felt proud of herself, knowing that this was what her mother would have done, knowing as well that her mother would have forgiven her the small lie about the tea. Their ration never seemed to last, as Colin was the only one who did not drink it. With a sweep of her hand, Ellen indicated the door to the parlor and ushered the stranger in. Colin tried to slink upstairs to his room, but Ellen was having none of that. Between clenched teeth, she hissed, "You keep our guest company, Colin, while I get the drinks."

In the kitchen, Ellen leaned against the big oak table and tried to calm herself. She had to find out just what Colin had been up to — and decide what to do about it. She hoped it was something minor, something that wouldn't send her father into one his rages that lasted for days and blighted the whole household. Ellen glanced over to the stove: the potatoes were still bubbling and the oven had reached temperature, so she could put in the steak and kidney pie. The table was a mess, covered with flour and scraps of pastry, but with luck she could get it cleaned up before her mother came home. Ellen placed three glasses on a tray, fetched the pitcher of lemonade from the icebox, placing over it a gauze cloth weighted with blue beads to keep out flies. There! Very elegant.

In the parlor, Colin and the stranger were sitting in silence, Colin sullen and the stranger ill at ease. When Ellen came in, the young man jumped to his feet and grabbed at the tray, almost causing her to drop it. "Let me do that," he said. "There's really no need to go to any trouble. I should be on my way."

Ellen placed the tray on the table in front of the large sateen-covered sofa. "It's no trouble, really, but —" she paused, "— it seems as if Colin has been."

The stranger picked up the cue, his words tumbling out in an untidy rush. "I was coming in to land, and I saw him and his friends running across the end of the runway by the fence." He smiled ruefully. "It gave me kind of a start, made me bugger up the landing. If they'd been any farther in I could have hit them."

Ellen gasped. Her father would have a blue fit when he heard.

The young man blushed, obviously misinterpreting her reaction. "Pardon my French, that just slipped out." He gave Colin a stern look, but it was soon replaced by a grin that made him look like a mischievous schoolboy. "Not all the other pilots are as good as me!" His smile faded. "The lads could cause someone to have a prang."

Colin had the grace to look shamefaced. "I was only trying to get a closer look. I didn't mean anything by it."

"Colin! You promised Dad you wouldn't go there at all. And now you've broken your promise and nearly caused an accident. And you could've got yourself killed! What were you thinking of?" Ellen couldn't control the exasperation in her voice. "Will he get into trouble up at the base?" Her heart almost stopped at the thought of the military police turning up on the doorstep. Dad would stay angry for months.

"Nah." The young man smiled, a shy smile. "I'm the only one what saw him. Once I collared him, I made him tell me where he lived. I reckoned it would be better if I just brought him home — let his family haul him over the coals." His smile broadened and his eyes got a faraway look. "At his age I was mad about planes, too. I used to spend all my weekends crouched at the end of the runways at Hendon Aerodrome, back home in London." He looked directly at Colin. "You didn't mean any harm, did yer, kid? And you'll never ever do it again, right?"

Colin nodded vigorously, but his hands were once again behind his back with his fingers crossed.

"Colin!" Ellen snapped, and pulled his hands forward. "This isn't a game. You were lucky this time. The gentleman's right. And if Dad should ever find out he'll take his belt to you ..." Ellen's voice trailed off as she saw a spark of genuine fear in her brother's eyes. Colin had only ever got the belt twice — and then only two strokes — but he'd seen Stewart and Graham get it often enough, and knew that he was old enough now to get the full works.

"Don't tell Dad," Colin pleaded, his voice sounding shaky.

Ellen looked at the young man. What would he think if she agreed? Did he want to see Colin punished? She sighed, "Well, if you really, truly promise, Colin, and you've got to mind what I say more than you do." Ellen glanced at the airman. He wasn't protesting, so she continued. "All right, I won't tell this time. But just this time, mind."

"Ellen, you're the best." Colin's fear was replaced by elation. He turned to his rescuer. "I watched you landing. It was amazing, the way it came down, and then went up, and then bumped down again." Using his hands, Colin re-enacted the plane's aborted landing, throwing in a few sound effects for good measure.

"Terrifying, rather than amazing. I don't think I've ever been so scared in my life." The young man shook his head. "Everyone in the plane was shouting instructions at me. Thought it was going to be the end of my flying career, I can tell you. Told 'em that a raccoon had startled me." His laugh sounded just a little too hearty as he stood up. "I'd better be going, now I've done what I set out to." He looked steadily at Ellen. "You make sure that this brother of yours keeps his word. He could get himself into a real scrape if he pulls a stunt like that again."

Ellen stood up to usher their guest out, relieved that everything had been sorted out, and wanting to get rid of him before either of her parents came home. "Thank you," she said. "I'll keep him out of trouble."

"Hey!" Colin was completely restored to good spirits. "You promised him some lemonade, Ellen, and you've not even offered any. It's a long walk back to camp, you know, unless someone gives him a ride." He turned to the airman. "While you drink it, you can tell me about flying. I'm going to be a pilot, too. I'll fly in the war just like you and my big brother, Graham. He's out at Trenton, going over to England soon. You're English, aren't you? I can tell by your accent." Colin was fizzing with excitement. "What's your name? You've not even told us that. I'm Colin Logan and this is my sister, Ellen."

Ellen tried to glare Colin quiet, but it didn't work. She shrugged and, raising her voice across Colin's chatter, said, "Would you like some lemonade?"

The young man ducked his head in assent, and blushed again. "I would, actually. I've got quite a taste for Canadian lemonade. It's nothing like the stuff back home." Awkwardly, he thrust his hand at Ellen. "I'm Stephen Dearborn. Pleased to meet you."

After shaking his hand, which felt sweaty and hot, Ellen busied herself pouring the cold drinks. There was no need for her to talk. Colin was doing enough for both of them, and Stephen was good-humoredly trying to answer the questions being fired at him.

Settling back into her chair, Ellen sipped the tart lemonade. She smiled — Barb and Deanna would be sick with envy if they could see her, entertaining a pilot in her parents' parlor. Most of the girls in town had been uniform crazy ever since the base opened almost two years ago. The foreign trainees were thought to be the most romantic, but Ellen had to admit that she didn't find Stephen particularly dashing. If anything, he was rather nondescript. His face was nothing special either, neither good-looking nor ugly. His only good feature as far as Ellen was concerned was his hair, which was a reddish brown and very wavy.

Ellen hadn't really been listening to Stephen and Colin, but she tuned in as Colin started to talk about Graham again.

Stephen sat upright. "That's who you thought I was!" he said to Ellen. "That's why you hugged me?"

Ellen felt her cheeks heat up again. "It's so embarrassing."

Stephen laughed. "Here I was bringing this little tyke home and a strange girl throws herself at me." He glanced at Ellen. "I'll be honest — nothing like that has ever happened to me before."

Ellen didn't know what to say, but was saved by Colin, who launched into a long and detailed account of Graham's flying training and how he was hoping to be sent to a fighter squadron in England.

Stephen shuddered. "He sounds brave, your brother. As far as I'm concerned, training can go on as long as it likes." He stopped himself abruptly. Then, realizing that both Colin and Ellen were staring at him, he said, "Did you say your dad was Scots, Colin?" Trying to sound casual, he added, "Do you still have relatives there?"

While Colin answered, Stephen's remark turned in Ellen's brain. What did he mean, he didn't want his training to end? She felt a surge of anger. Here he was, safe in Canada. She remembered how eagerly her brothers had signed up, going down to Hamilton the day Canada had declared war. Stewart hadn't even seemed to mind that his medical studies would be put on hold. He'd signed on with the army — the Royal Hamilton Light Infantry, and had been proud to do so. He wasn't a shirker. Shirker. The word was on the tip of her tongue, when she heard the front door open and her father's heavy footsteps in the hallway.

"Dad, Dad! Come and meet Stephen. He's in the RAF." Colin bounced out of the parlor and was tugging on his father's sleeve before he even had a chance to remove his hat.

Ellen groaned inwardly. How were they going to explain Stephen's presence?

"Pleased to meet you, Mr. Logan." Stephen was on his feet, offering his hand to Ellen's father. "Stephen Dearborn. Your son had a small tumble from his bike, and I brought him home. Your daughter was kind enough to offer me a cold drink before I set off back to the camp."

Smooth, Ellen thought, very smooth. She studied her father carefully. His eyes were tired, but he forced himself to smile. "A good Samaritan, eh, laddie? Perhaps we can return the favor. My wife will be home shortly, and she'd be after me if I didn't ask you for supper. We have two boys in the forces, and she always hopes that other families will take care of them for us." Mr. Logan paused, shaded his eyes with one large hand. "Though there's little chance of that for young Stewart." Like a dog coming out of water, he shook himself. "Ellen, before you set the table you might investigate what's stinking up the hallway."

Ellen leaped to her feet. The potatoes! The bloody potatoes must have burned dry!

TWO

1445326 LAC S. Dearborn
SFTS 16
Hagersville
Ontario
Canada

2nd of November, 1942

Dear Mum and Dorrie,

I am writing to you sitting on my bed. It's quiet here in the H-block. Most of the chaps have gone to the flicks to see *The Bride Came C.O.D.* It stars James Cagney. I know you like him, Dorrie. I thought about going, but decided to give it a miss and catch you up with all my news.

Please note the way I started this letter off. I didn't think there was any point in addressing it to Dad. I suppose he's still refusing to even look at my letters. I know I defied him, but what's done is done. I'd really like it if you could talk to him,

Dorrie. It would make me feel better. I don't expect him to write or anything, but it would make me rest easier. When he's in a mood, everyone knows about it, and it isn't fair that you should bear the brunt of something I've done.

I'm not sure that moving back to London was a good idea. I know the house has been repaired, but you would all be much safer down in Brighton with Auntie May. And it's not like she would begrudge you being there, being all alone since Uncle Len died and with Frank out in the Far East. I'm sure she was glad of the company. How's my lovely old Mick doing? Thanks for looking after him. Keeping a dog can't be easy. How is he when the bombs fall? I really miss the old fellow.

We get some English news over here, and they're still reporting air raids over London almost every night. But I don't know how accurate the Canadian papers are. To read them, we'll be marching into Berlin in a couple of months. Talk about being optimistic! If half of what they print is true, it'll all be over before I qualify. Seriously, though, I do worry about you all, particularly with Dad on nights. That shelter in the garden is horribly damp. It must really make your arthritis play up, Mum.

It's really odd here in Canada, seeing the houses all perfect and undamaged. I don't think people here realize what it's like for people back in Britain. Here, they think they have it hard because rationing has been introduced. I had to laugh the other day — one of the women at the Hostess House was complaining that no Huntley and Palmer biscuits will be imported from Britain until the war is over!

How's Andrew doing, Dorrie? I bet he misses Ron something rotten. A boy needs his dad. I know thousands of other children are in the same boat, but all the same.

Talking of Ron, I'm going to write to him as well. I know Ron's no great shakes as a letter writer, but could you ask him to write back to me sometime? Is Andrew still mad about planes? I've been thinking a lot about him in the last day or two because I met a Canadian lad who reminded me of him. This boy, Colin's his name, is a couple of years older, maybe nine, but he's lively like Andrew — a bit of a menace to tell the truth. I ended up escorting him from the base to his family in Hagersville and they insisted I stay for my tea, only they called it dinner.

You can't imagine how good it was to get off the camp, even for a couple of hours. I didn't realize how much I hate the smell here in the H-block — a mixture of paint, oil, cigarette smoke and disinfectant. The Logans' house — that's the kid's family — smelled like our home. Furniture polish and food cooking. I almost expected to see you coming out of the kitchen, Dorrie, wiping your hands on your pinnie, and you, Mum, lying on the sofa in the parlour.

I met the kid's sister first. Ellen, her name is. She's all right, I suppose, but we got off on the wrong foot. You'd have both laughed, but I was embarrassed. She just saw the uniform and threw her arms around me. Turns out she has an older brother in the RCAF, and she thought it was him come home on leave. I've never seen anyone go so red. Anyway, her dad invited me to stay for my tea.

He was a nice bloke, a Scot who came over after the last war. He was at the Somme like our Dad, but he talks about it and didn't mind me asking him questions, either. Mind you, he had enough questions for me, so it was only fair that he answered mine. His wife was the same when she turned up. Blimey, you would have thought I was on trial, all the stuff they wanted to know. Turns out they've got two boys in the forces. The RCAF one I was mistaken for — he's training up at Trenton, but he's going to be shipping out to England soon. I've given the Logans your address to pass on to him. Hope you don't mind. Maybe this Graham can look you up when he's in London, and you can treat him to some home cooking, too. It's got to be better than what they served up! That sounds ungrateful, and I don't mean it to. Only the daughter had done the cooking, see, and I reckon she needs a bit more practice. Her steak and kidney pie was all right (not a patch on yours, of course, Dorrie!), but she'd burned the potatoes. Have you ever had burned mashed potatoes? I wouldn't recommend them! Being a guest, I had to eat them. Young Colin, though, wasn't so polite. He nearly got a clip round the ear from his dad for being cheeky. His dad told him that he should be grateful that he'd got food on the table at all, that there were thousands over in Europe who hadn't. Mrs. Logan got a bit teary then and I didn't understand why. When she left the room to help Ellen bring in the pudding, Mr. Logan explained it all to me.

It turns out their other son, Stewart, was on the Dieppe raid in August. He was a stretcher bearer with (and this really threw me for a loop until he explained it) some regiment that he called the Rileys. Turns out that's the local regiment, the Royal Hamilton Light Infantry. Well, their son didn't come back and he's not shown up on any list as captured either. Imagine the worry! He's been missing for two months now. At least you know where we are: Ron down at Manston and me safe here in Canada.

Cor, this must be my longest letter ever. The Logans have invited me to Sunday dinner. Talk about kind, they've even moved their meal to late afternoon when my training's finished for the day. Let's hope Mrs. Logan does the cooking, not Ellen! I feel more cheerful than I've done for a long time. Keep smiling!

Your loving son and brother,
Stephen

P.S. Please try and talk Dad round, Dorrie.

✷   ✷   ✷

The huge wind howled past the fuselage of the plane, battering Stephen's ears and taking his breath away.

His face felt strange, too, as if it had been frozen, and now the skin at his temples and around his eyes was stretching tight. He had a desperate urge to go to the toilet; his bowels roiled and rumbled. The chaps would never let him live it down if he messed himself like a baby. Already they called him Swee'Pea after Popeye's baby, because he was the youngest on the course — if only they knew just how young he was. He shook himself as great waves of fear swept through him again. "Stupid!" he tried to yell, although his mouth didn't seem to be working properly. "You're in a spiral dive." The wind, the tightness in his face all made horrible sense. It was textbook, just like Warrant Officer Mackay had described to them back in the classroom.

Frantically, Stephen tried to remember what to do. He looked despairingly over his shoulder — maybe one of the other chaps would know. It was so odd, he thought. They should have been yelling at him by now, banging his shoulders. Lowther would normally have been grabbing at the stick, calling him a bloody idiot! Where were they all? He thought of Mackay again, tried to remember what he had told them to do. Stephen's mind was blank. He kept seeing Mackay's face, seeing his gingery handlebar mustache twitch as he smiled and said, "Ah, but none of my laddies are going to be fool enough to get themselves into a dive, are they?"

All the switches and dials in front of him meant nothing. Stephen looked down at his hands, clumsy in leather gauntlets, clutching the stick. Tentatively, he lifted one, watched how slowly it moved. The air had solidified and it took all his strength to push through it. He pulled hard back. Nothing happened.

The wind was getting louder. There was a metallic screaming that hurt Stephen's ears. At first he thought the plane was breaking apart, then he realized that he was making the noise, a high-pitched, keening wail that tore his throat. Through the windscreen of the cockpit, he could no longer see sky, just the brown and green blur of the ground that was hurtling toward him. Instinctively, Stephen threw his hands in front of his face, knowing, even as he did it, that it was useless. Nothing could save him now.

"Put a sock in it, Swee'Pea, for God's sake!"

Stephen was confused. Someone was shaking his shoulder roughly. He wasn't alone in the plane after all. He forced his hands down from his face. In the dim light of the barrack room, he could make out a figure bending over him. It was Lowther, the New Zealander who had the bunk above him. "You've been wailing like a bloody banshee for the last five minutes. We're trying to sleep. Mackay will be after us tomorrow if we're less than sharp. Now, shut it." With a last shake, Lowther scrambled up into his bunk, grumbling to himself.

Stephen lay unmoving, staring up at the bottom of Lowther's bunk, watching the thin mattress bulge and then flatten out as Lowther squirmed to get comfortable. His heart was racing and, despite the frigid air in the barrack room, he was sweating, so much that his flannel pajamas were sodden. He held his hand in front of his face, half surprised to see that it was ungloved. The nightmare had been so real.

Nothing was how he had thought it would be. Back in London, listening to his brother-in-law Ron's stories about life in the RAF, he'd thought it would be exciting and glamorous to be a pilot, to go out and blast the hell out of the Jerries.

Stephen shuddered and turned over so that he faced the wall. He closed his eyes, knowing that he wouldn't sleep. He promised himself that he would listen closely to Mackay in the morning and would memorize what to do if you got into a spiral dive.

☆　　☆　　☆

1445326 LAC S. Dearborn
SFTS 16
Hagersville
Ontario
Canada

3rd of November, 1942

Dear Ron,

Just a note to let you know that I'm fine. I've
written to Mum and Dorrie as well. It seems like
they're coping all right. Have you been able to get
up to see them since they came back to London?
How's the Old Man? Dorrie says he won't let
them mention my name. You'd think he'd be
pleased to have me serve my country. He did,
after all. I know he wanted me to have the
opportunities that he never had and was proud
that I got into Haberdasher Aske's school, but I
can pick all that up again once the war's over.
I just hope that Dorrie can bring him round.

More's to the point, how are things with you?
Are those bloody pilots still messing up your
aircraft? Careless buggers letting Germans shoot at
them and all that! They are just out to make work
for you ground-crew boys. Being shot at isn't
something I have to worry about yet. I have
enough trouble keeping my kite in the air. It all
looked so easy when you used to take me out to
the aerodrome at Hendon. I never realised how

hard those pilots had to work, and all the studying. Lucky maths and science come easy to me.

Talking of studying, I'd better pack this in. We're starting night flying tonight. I'm going to try and have a couple of hours kip so that I'm in tip-top form. Sleeping isn't always easy — you should hear some of the others snore! Last thing I want to do is wash out of the course.

If you can, write me how Mum and Dorrie are doing. I don't think they always tell me everything. Give Andrew a hug from his uncle.

Best wishes,
Stephen

P.S. Ron, one thing I wanted to ask you. Do you ever have, you know, nightmares?

THREE

There was a real bite to the air. First time this year, Ellen thought as she ran, clutching her books tightly to her chest. Barb and Deanna were waiting for her at Deanna's gate. Even at this distance, she could tell they weren't too pleased. It was always the same. Just when it was time for her to leave, there would be something: Colin would claim he couldn't find some item of clothing or his school satchel, or that his pants needed mending. She was sure he did it deliberately. In fact, she knew he did, because he smirked when their mother wasn't looking. It never failed, though. Mum would tell Ellen to help him, and Ellen always ended up keeping her friends waiting.

Sometimes, Ellen just couldn't make Colin out. Why did it amuse him so much to make her late? The little swine probably liked the sense of power it gave him. He knew that if Ellen protested, she would get a lecture about how everyone had to help out in wartime and Colin was too young to do things for himself. Ellen snorted. She just wished her parents could see Colin when he was out with his friends. He was never "just a little boy" then.

Deanna was already closing her gate when Ellen finally reached them, puffing slightly. "Don't tell us. Master Colin was up to his usual nonsense. He can be such a twerp. I don't know why your parents let him get away with it. If my sister tried any of his tricks, she'd get her legs slapped, that's for sure."

Deanna's words echoed Ellen's own thoughts, but she felt that it wasn't right for her friend to be so openly critical. "Mum and Dad have never really got over nearly losing him when he was just a little boy, when he had whooping cough so badly. Mum thinks he's still delicate."

"Delicate! Colin delicate?" Deanna spluttered. "Ask Barb's brother what he gets up to. Jeff's almost eleven and he's scared of Colin."

Barb nodded. "It's true, Ellen. Jeff says that Colin's really wild and that the other kids hang around with him just to see what he's going to get up to next. Colin and his gang have been building something out in the bush, some sort of camp or hideout. Jeff stopped going, because Colin said that kids could only come if they stole something from home for it, and Jeff wasn't going to do that."

Ellen sighed. That explained the mysterious disappearance of the saucepan in which she had burned the potatoes. She had left it soaking in the sink, but when her dad set out to tackle it with some steel wool, the saucepan was gone. He'd accused Ellen of throwing it out, even though she would never have done that and told him so. That didn't stop him lecturing her on how important it was not to waste things, especially with a war going on.

Barb linked one arm through Ellen's and the other through Deanna's as they set off down the road to school. The shortest of the three girls, she had to peer up at Ellen when she spoke. "I must say, Miss Logan," she said, doing her best to mimic an English accent, "you are looking particularly charming today. Would this ravishing coat you're wearing be the one about which we have heard so much?"

Ellen giggled. Barb could always make her laugh, or cheer her up when she was feeling miserable. In all her ruffled feathers about Colin, she had forgotten the coat. Extricating herself from her friends, she did a pirouette. "Do you like it?" Ellen ran her fingers over the smart, brass buttons and then stroked the soft fur collar.

"Like it?" Deanna's voice was incredulous. "I am green with jealousy. If I didn't know it was a hand-me-down, I might even hate you!"

Smiling at her friend, Ellen said, "It's okay, isn't it? When my auntie first offered it to me, I thought it would be dreadful. It was so old fashioned, and I drowned in it. The only good thing was that it was bright red. I mean, my dad would never let me choose a color like that." She lowered her voice in a passable imitation of her father's brogue. "Och, lassie, we canna have something so bright. We need something that

won't show the dirt, something serviceable. We need
a coat that will last you years. If it wasnae that your
auntie's giving it you for free ..."

Both Barb and Deanna had known Mr. Logan all
their lives, so they knew that Ellen was not
exaggerating her father's frugality and keen eye for a
bargain. They both laughed, and Ellen continued. "She
did it deliberately, you know, to get his goat. She knew
he couldn't refuse it, and she'd already made plans with
my mum about how she could alter it for me. So, for
once in my life, I have something halfway fashionable."

"Give us another twirl," Deanna commanded. "It is
lovely, Ellen," she said, when Ellen complied. "Your
mum's so clever, the way she's got it fitted on top, but
made its skirt swirl like that. Everyone says she's the
best seamstress in town."

Barb added, "It's a grown-up coat."

"She got the idea from a photograph in *Chatelaine*."
Ellen remembered how carefully her mother had fitted
the coat, for a while losing the worried look that
always seemed to haunt her eyes lately. They had even
laughed and joked as her mother recalled how she and
her sister had been the two best-dressed girls in
Dundas, thanks to their own skill, and how they had
gone promenading in Gore Park in Hamilton on
Sunday afternoons, pinching each other and giggling
when they caught young men giving them the eye. It
was there that she had met Billy Logan, out with his
mates from the steelworks. The men had competed to
make an impression on the two girls. Her mother had

liked the young Scotsman best, because he was the quietest, with a dignity that the others didn't have, and he had made her laugh with his dry observations about the others' foolishness. When he had asked if he could see her again, she'd said yes straight away. It was hard for Ellen to imagine her serious father making people laugh, let alone ever being called Billy.

"Oh, no!" Barb's sharp exclamation shattered Ellen's thoughts. "Just look at her. Who does she think she is?"

Following Barb's gaze, Ellen saw Patsy Grant near the school doors. By bending her knee and resting one foot against the wall, Patsy was standing in such a way that her tightly sweatered breasts were thrust forward, much to the delight of the group of boys paying court to her. Although she appeared to be listening to the boys, it was obvious to Ellen that Patsy was eyeing each person who arrived at school. When she spotted Ellen and her friends, she sauntered over, her blond sausage curls bouncing with each step. The boys milled around for a few seconds, but when Patsy paid them no more attention, they remained by the wall, contenting themselves with admiring the delicate and calculated sway of Patsy's rear.

"Well, hello ladies," Patsy's voice strained for an air of sophistication, but an unfortunate tendency to squeakiness spoiled the effect. "If it isn't the Andrews Sisters. Oh, dear, I've got it wrong. It's the Three Stooges."

"Yeah, we love you, too, Patsy." Deanna's height worked to her advantage, forcing Patsy to step back. "If you can't say anything nice, why don't you just skedaddle?"

Ignoring Deanna's hostility, Patsy fixed her eyes on Ellen. "Oh, so you want to keep the news all to yourself, do you?"

"News, what news?"

Normally Patsy never bothered to notice Ellen's existence, let alone talk to her.

"Aren't you the cute one, Ellen Logan, playing the innocent? Are you afraid that if anyone else is around, he won't bother with a dowdy little mouse like you?" Patsy looked Ellen up and down. "Although, I must say, you're a lot better dressed than normal. Amazing," she drawled, "what a boyfriend will do for a girl's confidence."

"Boyfriend!" Turning to Ellen, Deanna said almost accusingly, "What does she mean?"

"I've no idea." Ellen's voice sounded high pitched, and she could feel a flush rising in her face. "I haven't got a boyfriend. You know that." She looked pleadingly from Barb to Deanna, willing them to believe her, and to believe that she wouldn't keep something that important from them.

"Oh, then who was that handsome young pilot I saw going into your house yesterday?" Patsy's smile broadened and she moved so close Ellen could smell her sweet, minty gum. "Aren't you the sly one, landing one of the trainees and a Brit at that?"

Ellen felt the tension leave her. "That's just Stephen. He's not my boyfriend. He helped Colin." How could she say this without revealing exactly what Colin's escapade had been? Remembering Stephen's quick thinking, she stuck with that. "Colin fell off his bike and Stephen brought him home. He stayed for dinner that night, and then my mum asked him back for Sunday dinner as well." She laughed nervously. "That's all."

Deanna had a mulish look on her face. "Funny you didn't mention it till now, Ellen."

"Well, I've hardly had a chance, have I? This is the first time I've seen you, and all we've talked about is my coat. And then Patsy here starts trying to stir up trouble. Besides, it didn't strike me as all that interesting." Ellen looked at Deanna, watching the emotions flicker over her face. Deanna hated to be left out. "It was really dull, believe me. He's a real suck-up, this Stephen. Spent the whole time flattering my mother. 'Oh, Mrs. Logan, this reminds me of the meals my sister cooks at home. How do you get your potatoes so crisp?'" Ellen's oily imitation of Stephen seemed to do the trick. The corners of Deanna's mouth were turning up and Barb was giggling outright. Only Patsy looked unhappy.

"You're just saying that, Ellen Logan. I bet you were all over him." Patsy made one last attempt. "He looked a bit of a dreamboat to me."

"Dreamboat!" Ellen's voice was loud. "You need to get your eyes checked, Patsy. He's got pimples, he's not very tall and he looks worried all the time." Ellen stood up straighter. "We're not all like you, going all goo-goo-eyed at the sight of a uniform, whatever's inside it." Then with the slightest hint of a smile, she added, "Hung around any good gates lately, Patsy?"

Without a word, Patsy flounced back to her waiting admirers. When one of them spoke to her, she snapped at him, then smiled as the boy flushed a deep crimson. She made a point of not looking over at Ellen, Deanna and Barb.

"Well, you certainly told her off!" Barb's voice was admiring. "But it can't have been all that bad, Ellen. It must have been interesting to hear about England."

Ellen didn't have time to answer, as the students were jostling their way inside the building, but later that day in Geography, when Mr. Jones was droning on about how they should make their maps neater, Ellen found herself thinking about Stephen.

He had arrived earlier on Sunday than they had expected, clutching a handful of leaves, burrs and milkweed pods that he had fashioned into a rough bouquet. As soon as he saw her mum, he'd thrust them awkwardly at her, muttering about how he would have liked to have given her real flowers, but hoped she might like the colors in the leaves he had found. Ellen had had to kick Colin to stop him giggling. Stephen's bumbling gesture had set the tone for the whole visit. He was like an overgrown puppy, eager to please but not quite sure how to do it. Everything was proclaimed to be wonderful, and if he had thanked them for inviting him once, he must have done it twenty times. Ellen smiled remembering how Colin had caught her eye and pretended to vomit when Stephen was praising their mother's very ordinary apple pie.

Stephen was rather pathetic, really, and not at all how she had imagined a pilot would be. Her brother Graham had taken her to see *The Dawn Patrol*, and the stars of that film, Errol Flynn and David Niven, with their quick wit, handsome faces and dashing manner had become her idea of what an RAF pilot should be. She suppressed a giggle. That film had caused a lot of trouble, because it had convinced Graham that flying was what he wanted to do. There had been a terrible ruckus when their dad had discovered that Graham had drawn all the money out of his savings account to pay for flying lessons at Mount Hope. Mind you, it had paid off. When war was declared, Graham had had no trouble getting into the RCAF.

Ellen suddenly became aware that the room had gone silent. Raising her head, she realized that everyone was looking at her — including Mr. Jones, whose lips were compressed into a thin, annoyed line.

"Am I boring you, Miss Logan?" The precisely enunciated words carried through the silence.

Ellen, swallowing hard, stuttered, "N-n-no. I'm sorry, sir."

Softening his glare, Mr. Jones continued. "Well, such inattention is definitely out of character, Ellen. Just turn to page thirty-seven in your atlas, like everyone else did some time ago, and start on your map. We'll let this little lapse go."

"She has other things on her mind," Patsy Grant pretended to whisper, but everyone heard. "Like a boyfriend."

Ellen clenched her teeth and concentrated on drawing the map of Canada. Stephen Dearborn was becoming a nuisance.

FOUR

1445326 LAC S. Dearborn
SFTS 16
Hagersville
Ontario
Canada

15th November, 1942

Dear Mum and Dorrie,

Thank you for your letters. They really cheered me up. I hadn't had a letter for a while, and I was getting a bit down. Then I got five in one bundle. I should know by now not to expect things to run smoothly. There is a war going on, after all. Ha, ha! Once I'd sorted them out into order, I had a really good read.

I especially liked Andrew's drawing of me standing by my plane. Tell him to make the "kite" yellow next time, a really bright yellow, just like

Bird's Custard Powder when you add milk to it. All the training planes are that colour. I thought it was so we'd be easy to spot and avoid when we're in the air. But one chappie told me that yellow makes the wreckage easier to find when we crash. I reckon it's being so cheerful that keeps him going! I'll just have to make sure I don't put his theory to the test.

Anyway, tell Andrew that the drawing was much appreciated. It gave the others a chuckle, too, because he had made me so tall. Well, here, I'm the titch of the course, and don't they give me what for about it — all in fun, of course. One chap, Lowther, is a bit of a card. He's got the bunk above me and he's got this routine that he does. Sometimes, if I say something, he'll ask, "Did anyone hear a noise, bit like a mouse squeaking?" Then he'll act all surprised and notice me, doing a big double take like someone in a comedy flick. "Oh, my goodness, it's young Master Dearborn. Sorry, Stephen, didn't notice you down there." The first time, I wasn't sure how to take it, but he means no harm and we all need a good laugh. They've re-christened me "Swee'Pea" after Popeye and Olive Oyl's baby, because I'm the baby of the course. Everyone's got a nickname except one chap no one likes — he's always complaining. Everyone just calls him by his name, that's if they can't ignore him. Anyway, I can live with Swee'Pea. It could have been much worse. There's one bloke called Durrant and they call him "The Schnozz," after some Yankee comedian, Jimmy Durante, who's famous for his big nose. Lowther's nickname is "Kiwi," because he's from New Zealand. As to being small, at five foot, six inches, I'm the ideal height and build for a pilot. That's what our instructor, Warrant Officer Mackay, said. Some of the bigger chaps have a devil of a time inside a plane. Lowther's given his head a right crack more than once.

I've rambled on, haven't even asked how you're doing. That cold you've got, Mum, sounds nasty. Make sure you wrap up warm of an evening, especially when you're in that blasted shelter. I can't believe Mick doesn't bark during a raid. Maybe the poor old boy's too scared. It made me smile to hear that he and Andrew snuggle up together.

The weather's getting colder here, although we haven't seen any snow yet. The Logans, the family I told you about in my last letter, have been telling me what to expect. I think they're having a laugh at my expense. I can't believe it gets as cold as they say. I've been to their house a couple of times since I last wrote. When we have free time, a lot of the Canadians head off to Hamilton. Some have friends or family there. Others go for the bars and the dances. They always ask us Brits to go out with them. I'm not a drinker — I'm like the

Old Man that way. I always think of the state that
Auntie Vi and Uncle Tom used to get into and
how they used to leave their kiddies hanging
around outside the pub. It really turns me off the
whole idea of drink. The Logans told me to come
to them any time I was free. I didn't like to at
first, but I was so brassed off last Saturday when I
thought you'd all forgotten me (just kidding!) that
I took them at their word.

When I arrived I found their oldest son there,
on embarkation leave before he shipped out to
England. I didn't want to intrude, but they insisted
that I stay and I'm glad. It became a right old
knees-up. Mrs. Logan's sister and family were
there and Graham, the son, had asked some of his
friends over, plus a whole load of people from
town. The only one who was a bit off was the
girl, Ellen. She hardly spoke two words to me the
whole time I was there. I can't for the life of me
think how I offended her — I even asked her kid
brother what was up. He just laughed and said to
ignore her, she could be a right stuck-up little
madam at times. Well, I did, but, you know me, I
hate any unpleasantness.

Mr. Logan got the whisky out to toast Graham
on his way. He and the men were giving him
advice and they tried to get me to tell Graham
where to go in London. All I could do was repeat
things I'd heard from Ron and the others. What a

sheltered life I've led. Here I am in Canada, a whole big ocean away. Me, who'd rarely been out of South London.

Anyway, I don't think Graham Logan's going to be homesick. I've never met anyone with such confidence, bags of it he has, and some to spare. He's nothing like Ellen, who's quiet like a little mouse. Their mum told me that Ellen was closest to her other brother, Stewart — the one who's missing. "Bookish" was how she described them. Remember Dad saying the same about me? Only he didn't mean it as a compliment!

Talking of the Old Man, Dorrie, any joy on that front? Do you show him my letters or not bother?

Well, look at all these pages. Perhaps I should take this writing lark up after the war. It just seems to flow once I get started, and it does take my mind off things.

Your loving son and brother,
Stephen

P.S. I had a letter from Alan Grainger, in the same lot as yours. I presume he got my address from you when he was home on leave. Thanks, I'll write to him, although whether it will reach him, I don't know, since his unit's on the move.

★   ★   ★

1445326 LAC S. Dearborn
SFTS 16
Hagersville
Ontario
Canada

15th of November, 1942

Dear Alan,

Just a quick note to let you know I'm still in the land of the living. I hate to think where you are now. A cushy leave like you had normally means they're going to send you somewhere nasty!

We have it really easy here. All the food we can eat, no one shooting at us (yet) and the chance to fly, just like we always talked about when we were at school. Shame you aren't in the RAF, too. What a pair we'd have made!

I like it here in Canada. The people are really friendly, and it's not like back home where people judge you by who your family is. Do you remember how those snot-noses at school looked down on us because we were scholarship boys? Didn't matter that we had the brains to get there. All that counted was that we didn't have money like they did. It used to really get my goat, especially because I could never talk about it to Dad, Mum or Dorrie; they were all so proud of me, especially the Old Man. There are some public school types here on the course, but we're all in the same boat, struggling to master the trickier bits of flying and get our wings.

I should be finished here at the end of February. Don't know where they'll send me. I think I'll be based in England, flying into Europe. If you can trust the newspapers, that's where the next push will be. I can't say I'm looking forward to that.

You know how we used to dream about flying? Well, I'm going to let you in on a little secret, Alan, old boy. It's not all it's cracked up to be. Oh, it's thrilling at times, all that power and you controlling it. You do feel like an eagle, soaring above the clouds. Only trouble is, there's all the book work they make us do, and they even have us square bashing. We've got this flight sergeant who just loves to have us march up and down for hours on end. I ask you, what's the point? Marching drills aren't going to make us fly any better.

So, from your letter it sounds like you were getting all hot and heavy with Sybil Fisher on your last leave, but then you were always a bit of a ladies' man. Some Canadian girls are "uniform crazy." You should see the reception we get if we venture into town. Being so good-looking (joke), I'm having to fight them off! No, to be serious, I don't see the point. We're going to be shipped out in a couple of months anyway. And where would I ever find one who's as good a cook as Dorrie?

Hope this letter finds you safe,
Stephen

FIVE

Did he never stop talking? Ellen glanced at Stephen as he walked, oblivious to her annoyance, next to her.

Colin was just as bad, encouraging him with questions. In fact, it was all Colin's fault that she had been stuck with Stephen this afternoon. If he hadn't been his usual annoying self, dawdling and messing around, they would have left for the church's Christmas bazaar before Stephen turned up unexpectedly, saying that he had the rest of the afternoon off.

She had cringed when Colin had leaped all over Stephen, telling him of their plans and begging him to come with them. Ellen had hoped that her mother, who was stuck at home with a cold, would suggest that Stephen stay and chat to her. She never seemed to tire of talking to him about her sons and hearing all about life in England. But oh, no, she had just smiled fondly and said, "What a good idea, Colin. You and Ellen can introduce Stephen to your friends." There had been no point protesting, not when Stephen had seemed so pathetically eager. Ellen did a quick count of who might be there. Barb and Deanna definitely — they had made arrangements to meet. Probably just about everyone. It wasn't like there was that much else to do on a cold, rainy Saturday afternoon. All she could hope for was that Patsy wouldn't be there. A day hadn't gone by without some snippy remark from Patsy Grant. Ellen sighed.

"Penny for them?" Stephen broke off the description of night flying that he had been giving Colin. When Ellen didn't answer, not realizing he was speaking to her, he tried again. "Penny for them, Ellen — your thoughts. That was a deep old sigh!"

"Oh, nothing really." She couldn't tell him the truth. "I was just thinking how dull you're going to find this. It'll be the usual stands — bric-a-brac, used clothes, a cake stall, used books and magazines."

"Nah, you've got me all wrong." Stephen winked at her. "I bet you think I'm some kind of city slicker just because I come from London, but I'm not really. I only ever went to the center of London once, and that was to join up at the Air Ministry in Holborn. All those stories I was telling your dad and his friends was just a load of old flannel, stuff I'd picked up from the other chaps." He paused. "Besides, a break from routine, anything that's different, is a treat. I get so fed up, stuck on that base all the time." His face had become serious, but brightened as a thought occurred to him. "Did you say books?"

Ellen nodded.

"That's a bit of all right. I'm not a big filmgoer. I prefer to read of the evenings, but it's hard finding stuff." Stephen grinned and colored slightly. "Well, suitable stuff. You don't even want to think about some of the magazines that are lying about. They'd make your hair curl!"

Ellen let Stephen's words wash over her as she peered at the parish hall, trying to make out whether the figures by the door were her friends. Why did Stephen talk so much, she wondered? Give him an opening and he just went on and on. Was it nerves, or was he always like this?

Satisfied that Patsy Grant was not in sight, Ellen turned her attention back to Stephen, who was still talking.

"I asked my sister, Dorrie, to send some books over, but I don't like to do that too often. She's got enough on her plate, looking after our mum and her own son. Anyway," Stephen laughed, "her taste in books isn't exactly mine. She sent me over some Ethel M. Dell and Warwick Deeping. I didn't half get a ragging from the others about those 'soppy romances,' as they called them. But you know what? They read them!"

Ellen smiled. It did make a funny picture — all those manly pilots reading the type of books her mother cried buckets over.

"That's better!"

Startled, Ellen asked, "What do you mean?"

"The smile. That's about only the second time I've

ever seen you smile." Stephen smiled back at her and Ellen noticed how tired he looked, and the dark circles under his eyes.

"Oh, you shouldn't take it to heart," she said. "Graham, Colin and Mum are the cheerful ones. Mum says Stewart, Dad and I are moody, but we're just quiet, that's all."

Colin, who had been kicking a pebble along, let out a yell. "Look, there's Jeff." He pelted off down the road, leaving Ellen and Stephen far behind.

The hall was packed. Ellen was just able to catch a glimpse of Colin with a gaggle of friends, including Barb's brother, standing engrossed by a homemade ring-toss stand. She was about to tell Stephen that he needn't feel obliged to stay with her, when she felt a tug on her sleeve. Barb and Deanna had wormed their way over to her. Both of them were really dressed up and Deanna had on what looked suspiciously like Tangee lipstick. She must have sneaked it on after she left home — her mother would never have allowed it.

"So, Ellen, you made it." Barb was studiously not looking too obviously at Stephen, as was Deanna.

Ellen wanted to laugh. Poor Barb almost looked as if she had a nervous tic, scrunching up her eyes to look sideways. It would be mean to let them continue. "Barb, Deanna, let me introduce you to Stephen Dearborn." She was amazed to see Deanna blush as Stephen shook her hand. "Stephen, these are my best friends from school, Barb Gannon and Deanna Reilly."

"We've heard such a lot about you, Stephen," Deanna said.

Ellen gasped. What was Deanna playing at? She had hardly ever mentioned Stephen, except, perhaps, to complain about how often he turned up. Now, he'd get a completely wrong impression!

"All of it good, I hope?" Stephen was smiling, and Barb and Deanna were just lapping it up. "I can't say that Ellen has said much about you two. She's not the most talkative of people, is she?"

"She can be, when she wants to be." Barb was getting in her two cents' worth, talking about her as if she wasn't there.

"Shall we have a look around?" Ellen knew she sounded abrupt, but she wanted to stop this silly chatter.

"Why not?" Stephen took her arm. "Perhaps you can show me the book stall you were talking about. And, if your friends would like to join us, maybe you'd all let me treat you to tea and a sticky bun over there." Stephen had spotted the corner of the hall where the Ladies Auxiliary had set out tables and chairs and were serving refreshments. "Shall we meet up there in twenty minutes?"

"Ooh, yes!" Deanna's eyes shone with pleasure. "Won't we create a stir!"

Ellen rolled her eyes. The afternoon was going from bad to worse.

In the end, Ellen had to drag Stephen away from the book stall, so engrossed had he become. She had been tempted not to, but her friends were already sitting at a table and their efforts to attract her attention had been getting more and more frantic. Stephen had surprised her. The reverence with which he handled the books — even the dusty, dog-eared old ones — was touching. His choices, too, had not been what she had expected. She had thought he would go for thrillers, or magazines. Instead, he had bought an old copy of a book of Rupert Brooke's poetry, some Shakespeare and, most surprising of all, a copy of *The Wind in the Willows.*

While Stephen busied himself getting tea and cakes, Deanna leaned over to Ellen. "He's quite dreamy, Ellen." She grinned. "Well, except for the pimples. Nowhere near as bad as you made out."

Ellen sniffed. "Deanna Reilly! You were flirting like crazy with him. I'm being mean about him, I know. It's just that he's always here, and Stewart isn't." Ellen felt a sob rising in her throat, and fought it down.

"That sounds really pathetic, but I can't help it. I keep wondering where Stewart is — in a prisoner-of-war camp, or …" Ellen couldn't say any more, trapped with the awful feeling that if she put her thought into words, it might become reality.

Deanna hugged her. "You'll get news sometime soon. You have to. It's been nearly three months now — he'll turn up." She exchanged a look with Barb over Ellen's bowed head. "It's not really fair to take it out on this guy. He's obviously just lonely and homesick. And you can't blame him for being here." Deanna shuddered. "And it's not like it's forever. He'll have worse to face soon enough."

Ellen knew that Deanna was right. She would try to be nicer to Stephen. He wasn't that bad, really, just a bit annoying, like a puppy that kept begging for attention.

She put her new resolve into practice immediately, jumping up to help Stephen with the teas as he returned to their table. "This is really very kind of you," she said.

"I've had enough meals at your place, Ellen. It's time I treated you." Stephen kept his eyes on the tray.

As they ate and drank, Ellen noticed that with Deanna and Barb around, Stephen seemed more relaxed, and didn't talk half as much. It suddenly occurred to her that perhaps his incessant chatter had been a nervous attempt to fill her silence.

"My, oh my! Swee'Pea has got himself a harem!" The voice came from behind Ellen, so she couldn't see its owner, but Stephen went scarlet.

"Aren't you the sly dog?" A tall, gangly man in an RAF uniform snagged a chair from a nearby table and placed it next to Ellen, its back touching the table so he could straddle it. He pushed back his cap and said, "You don't mind if we join you, do you?" as two other airmen dragged up chairs and squeezed around the small table. "Or are you intent on keeping these beauties all to yourself, Swee'Pea?"

The speaker was movie-star handsome, with a big, dashing mustache that twitched as he flashed a smile round the table. Barb and Deanna both went quite pink.

"Leave it out, Lowther!" Stephen's own blush was subsiding now. "This is Ellen," he said, indicating her, "the daughter of the family I've been visiting. The ones I told you about who've been so kind to me."

"Charmed, I'm sure." Lowther had a twangy accent, and Ellen had to suppress a giggle, so elegant was the way he shook her hand. For one awful moment, she thought he was going to kiss it! His eyes glittered with amusement, and Ellen hoped that Barb and Deanna realized that he was just having a lot of fun. Ellen had often been the recipient of this type of playful flattery from Stewart and Graham's friends.

"What are you doing here, anyway?" Stephen was grinning. "I thought an old sinner like you wouldn't dare show his face anywhere near a church."

"Ah, my boy! One has to keep tabs on the adversary." Lowther pretended to scan the hall.

"Ignore him, Dearborn." One of the other airmen spoke up for the first time. "We're all going in to Hamilton. We're catching the bus at Courtnage's, but since we had some time to kill, we thought we'd pass it here." He looked the girls over and obviously liked what he saw. Barb noticed his look, and casually tossed her long, blond hair off her face with a shake of her head. "You and your friends are welcome to join us. We're going to try out a dance hall called The Kensington."

Barb and Deanna were unable to speak for the

giggles, although it was very flattering to be thought old enough to go to dance halls. Ellen was saved from having to answer by Lowther, who rose languidly. "No, Evans, we're cramping Swee'Pea's style and he was here first. So, we shall leave him and his fair ladies in peace." He reached for Barb's hand and, this time, did kiss it, and then Deanna's. Their giggles got louder. Under the cover of this noise, when Lowther came to kiss Ellen's hand, he pretended to stumble, righting himself by leaning one hand on her shoulder, and whispered so that only she could hear, "Look after young Stephen. He's something of a little lost lambie!"

✳   ✳   ✳

Lowther's words reverberated in Ellen's head on the walk home. Just what did he mean? "A lost lambie." It made her think of the old poem her father liked so much, "Gentlemen Rankers," by Kipling. Whenever there was a family gathering, he recited it as his party piece, just as Ellen's mother always sang "Silver Threads Among the Gold." Ellen couldn't remember all the words, but there was a kind of chorus that was repeated. "We're three little lambs who've lost our way. We're little black sheep who've gone astray." Stephen certainly wasn't a black sheep — at times, he seemed so innocent that Ellen felt older than he was. But lost? Ellen glanced sideways at Stephen. He and Colin were exchanging friendly insults. How could he be lost, when he was living out his dream — being paid to learn to fly?

"Who's that?" Colin's question shook Ellen out of her reverie and she followed his pointing finger. A car was parked outside their house, its engine running. A tall, stooping figure was coming through their front door. As they drew nearer, Ellen saw her parents crowded into the doorway. Her father had one arm around her mother's shoulders, while he shook the visitor's hand with the other. Ellen's mother was dabbing at her eyes with a handkerchief.

Hardly daring to breathe, Ellen started to run, staring at the stranger. When she realized that he was not in uniform, relief raced through her. It wasn't someone from Stewart's regiment come with the news they had all been dreading. Whoever he was had his back to her, but there was something familiar about him.

Colin streaked past her and came to a quivering halt as the stranger turned toward them. Ellen stopped, too, just managing not to cry out.

A gargoyle's face solemnly regarded her. A scar ran from forehead to chin, pulling the left eye askew, its lids and rims red and sore looking. The eye was gray and cloudy like the ice that formed in puddles. The clear hazel iris of the other eye sparkled at Ellen.

"Robbie?" Ellen could manage only a whisper. Stewart's best friend.

"Ellen!" The voice was just as she remembered, a light baritone that had always sounded on the verge of laughter or good-natured teasing. Now it had a pleading quaver to it. "I can't be looking that bad, if you can still recognize me."

"I knew it was you right away." Ellen hoped she wasn't blushing the way she usually did when she lied. "Colin, you recognized Robbie, didn't you?" Ellen turned to Colin at her side. "That's why you ran so fast."

Colin was white-faced. His wide eyes were fixed on the ruin of Robbie's face. His mouth opened, but no sound came out until he burst into noisy, gulping sobs and ran for the back of the house.

No one said anything. Ellen looked at her parents, but their grim faces told her that they would be no help.

Ellen felt rather than saw Stephen push past her, thrusting his hand out to Robbie. "Hello, I'm Stephen Dearborn. I'm training at the flying school just outside town."

Stephen's everyday words, the aching ordinariness with which he delivered them, worked like magic, unfreezing everyone from their shock at Colin's outburst. Introductions were made and Robbie and Stephen chatted briefly until, nodding at the still-running car, Robbie said, "I've really got to go. My friend was kind enough to use some of his gas ration to get me here, but he's got to get back for work." He shook everyone's hand again, and added, "I just wanted to tell you all that when I last saw Stewart, he was alive. I'm sure you'll hear something soon."

Robbie patted Ellen's arm awkwardly, then glanced away. Colin's head reappeared around the corner of the house, his eyes almost swollen shut with crying.

Turning to the car, Robbie stumbled. He angrily motioned away the supporting hand that Stephen instinctively offered. Breathing heavily, he took the few steps to the curb, his face contorted with pain. What Ellen had not noticed before was now apparent. Robbie's left arm dangled uselessly and he dragged his left leg, its foot turned at an odd angle.

After Robbie's departure, Stephen made a few halfhearted protests that about leaving the Logans to their privacy, saying that he was sure they would want to talk about Stewart. But Mrs. Logan would have none of it. Ellen sighed. It looked as if Stephen had become a fixture that she would just have to get used to.

Talk of Stewart did dominate the dinner table, at least for Ellen's mother. She was happier than Ellen had seen her for a long time, smiling as she served up carrots and corned beef hash. She told Ellen the rest of what Robbie had said — how, while convalescing, he had asked other survivors of Dieppe if they knew what had happened to Stewart. "And do you know, Ellen, not one person saw him wounded!"

Ellen tried to smile, but she remembered the newspaper reports of the first news about Dieppe. So few had made it back safely, and they might not have been anywhere near Stewart. She knew that the padre, Canon Foote, who had been working with Stewart and the other stretcher bearers, had been captured. So maybe Stewart had, too. It just seemed so strange — nearly three months and they still had no news.

Colin's face still showed tearstains, but no one

mentioned his outburst. Her father was quiet until Stephen asked whether Stewart had known Robbie before the war. "Oh, aye," Ellen's father said, "they were at university together, but no one could stop them from throwing it all up to enlist."

"He seemed a nice chap," Stephen said. Ellen noticed him shiver slightly, that odd little shiver that people often say means someone is walking over your grave.

"Oh, he is," Mrs. Logan joined in. "When he and Stewart were training, he often spent his leave with us, didn't he, Ellen?"

Ellen didn't see why her mother was dragging her into this conversation, but she smiled and nodded. Robbie and Stewart had always had time for her and Colin, unlike Graham, who said they were annoying pests.

"He was a great athlete, was young Robbie." Her father's voice cut into Ellen's thoughts. "They still talk about the grand slam he hit when he played for our town baseball team back in 1940. I think he had dreams of playing professionally at one time." His face darkened. "No hope now. He told us all about it before you got back, Ellen. He and some others were sheltering behind a burned-out tank on the beach, when it took a direct hit. He was lucky to survive and not lose his leg." Mr. Logan stared at his water glass.

Ellen looked at Colin. Robbie had been his hero. A tear trickled down his face, but he made no sound.

"What will he do?" Stephen looked worried. "It must be dreadful to have your dreams dashed."

Ellen's mother smiled at him and offered him some

more carrots. "It'll be hard, I'm sure, Stephen, but Robbie's lucky in one way. His family has a manufacturing business in Toronto. He can go into that." Sensing that this answer didn't satisfy Stephen, she tried something to lighten the subject. "The way you talk about dreams, Stephen, I'll bet you have one."

Stephen looked down at his plate. When he raised his eyes, his face was more animated than Ellen had ever seen it. "I do." He paused, almost as if he were reluctant to share it. "I want to be a teacher."

Ellen sat up straight in surprise. Before she thought, she said, "Why, that's what I want to do!"

Laughter burst from her father. "Ellen, Ellen, where do you get such ideas?" He turned to his wife. "Have you heard the like before? Ellen wants to be a teacher."

Ellen was bewildered. She didn't understand why her father found this so funny. She had never said so, except to Stewart, but it was what she had wanted to do, ever since she could remember.

She pitched her voice low, trying to impress on him her sincerity. "I want to go to university, just like Stewart, and then teach English."

Mr. Logan straightened up, his laughter dying away. "Ellen, my dear, I don't doubt that you're serious, but it's unrealistic. Why would we waste money on sending you to university when you'll just get married and raise children?"

Ellen felt as if her father had punched her in the stomach. She found it difficult to breathe, let alone speak. She looked at her mother for support, but she had busied herself spooning vegetables onto her plate and would not meet Ellen's eyes.

"Mr. Logan," Stephen's voice was soft, but he smiled at Ellen, a fleeting smile that no one else saw, "girls do go to university now. I'm sure Ellen would do well, if she had a chance. " He quickly stared down at his plate, as if shocked by his own bravery.

"Laddie, I'm sure they do, if their families have got money to burn, but we haven't." Mr. Logan's voice was no longer jocular, and his accent was getting thicker as he enunciated his words clearly. "Ellen should know that without being told." He looked sharply at her. "I'm surprised that she would have such selfish thoughts, anyway. All you young men aren't being forced to put your dreams on hold by the war just so some flighty girls can take your places."

Ellen flinched, waiting for the explosion.

"Ellen might think less about herself, and more about what she could be contributing to the war effort." Her father's voice was controlled, but getting louder. "In fact, at work I heard of something that would suit you down to the ground, Miss Ellen Logan. If a girl's got good marks, she can leave school at fifteen to take up war work. I was going to discuss it with you, Ellen, but we'll just agree that you'll do it. Next November, on your birthday — that's when you'll leave school."

Ellen felt herself tremble. Her father was staring at her, waiting for her reaction.

"Well?"

"William, you're being very harsh on her," Ellen's

mother risked saying.

"Harsh!" Mr. Logan stood up. "Harsh is Stewart missing before his twenty-first birthday. Harsh is Robbie Morgan crippled for life. Harsh is young men like Graham and young Stephen here risking their lives for spoiled girls like her." He slammed his fist on the table, making the crockery jump and rattle.

Ellen felt herself rising from her seat. She had no idea what she was doing. All she knew was that she had to get away before she started to cry.

She heard her father say, "Leave her, Agnes. Don't go after her!"

Then Stephen's voice, shaky but determined. "I'll go and see if she's all right."

SIX

1445326 LAC S. Dearborn
SFTS16
Hagersville
Ontario
Canada

1st of December, 1942

Dear Mum and Dorrie,

Well, here I am in the snowy north, all right.
All flying's been canceled today because of high
winds and heavy snow. And let me tell you, the
Logans weren't exaggerating one bit. We had our
first snow on Saturday, and it's played havoc with
our flying training. The wind's the worst — cuts
through you like a blooming knife. Our flying suits
and jackets help a bit, but we can't wear them
indoors. The H-block is bitter. You asked me what
an H-block is. Sorry, I should have explained that,

it's the standard building on RAF bases. Two long wings, like the uprights of the letter H, contain the dormitories and living areas. The bit that connects them, the bar of the H, is where we have our ablutions as they so nicely call them — bathrooms to you and me, although you can imagine what they're like with so many of us using them!

Your letters were really welcome, because with no flying we've been hanging around once ground school is over for the day. Since the heavy snow started, I've been stuck here. A card school's got going. They're not meant to gamble, but they do, of course. I don't want to risk my money like that. I'm going to need every penny after the war for university. So, with nothing much to do, this is probably going to be my longest letter yet!

I couldn't help feeling guilty, Dorrie, reading about how you have to queue for your rations. The shortages sound really bad. You wouldn't believe the food here. Our food is like a feast with us as the kings. Civilians' food is rationed, but nowhere near as bad as you have it, and there always seems to be a way round, if you get my meaning. Mrs. Logan was telling me that the butcher asked her if she was entertaining "that boy in blue" again, and found her some extra meat. That made me feel better, I can tell you, because I've been feeling guilty about eating with them so often when they have to make do with rations. Whenever I can, I take something over, usually some sweets (or should I say candy?), for young Colin.

I might not visit them so often, anyway, even though it's being with a family that's helped me cope. Last time I was over, there was a to-do between Ellen and her dad, and it left me feeling a bit awkward.

It was Saturday, the last time I got off the base. I went over there after lunch. Ellen and Colin were going to their church's Christmas bazaar, so I tagged along. You would have laughed. Take away the funny accents and it was just like stepping into the church hall in New Cross. The stalls were set around the walls, just like home, and there was a woman serving teas who was the spit of Mrs. Partridge next door, even down to the silly hat! I half expected to see you running the white-elephant stall, like you used to do, Mum, before your arthritis got so bad.

We met up with some of Ellen's friends and they were a right laugh. One of them, I swear, was giving me the eye. Anyway, Lowther and his cronies turned up, and didn't they create a kerfuffle! The girls here certainly do pay attention to a chap in a uniform. (Yes, even me, your plug-ugly little brother, Dorrie.) Lowther looks a bit like Clark Gable, only thinner, and he can lay the charm on with a trowel. And Evans asked me and the girls if we wanted to go to a dance hall in

Hamilton! He didn't realize that Ellen and her
friends are only fourteen. Later, he just laughed
and said, "That blond piece" — that's Ellen's
friend, Barb — "is going to be a real bombshell!"
And it got worse. "Your girlfriend isn't too bad
either, if you can get past the freckles!" You can
bet I put him straight on that sharpish. Ellen, my
girlfriend, indeed!

Oh, I nearly forgot. They had a book stall and
I stocked up, so don't worry about looking out
for more stuff for me. I got some plays and poetry
and, just for old time's sake, *The Wind in the
Willows*. Dorrie, do you remember Dad reading it
to us in the garden — him in that old deck chair
and us sitting on the steps?

Reading it again is almost like being at home.

When we got back to the Logans', I was
hoping to stay for my tea. Mrs. Logan had invited
me before we set off, but they had a visitor, so
I was all set to hotfoot it back to camp. Their
visitor, a chap named Robbie, is a university
friend of their son Stewart. The two were in the
same regiment, and Robbie had got shot up
pretty badly. He looked a right mess. His face all
scarred, blind in one eye, his left side damn near
useless. Young Colin took one look at him and
scarpered, sobbing. Ellen's parents were speechless.
Ellen, I have to give it to her, she did her best.
She just tried to act like normal, but he knew it
was a struggle, and the last thing he wanted was

their pity and he left.

So I did stay for dinner, but it was pretty gloomy. They were telling me about what a good athlete Robbie had been, that sort of thing. The only one who was cheerful was Mrs. Logan. She'd convinced herself that because Robbie hadn't seen their Stewart wounded or killed, he must be all right. Anyway, I'm rambling on and I can just hear you, Mum, saying, "Get to the point, Stephen!"

I made some remark about Robbie's smashed dreams and Mrs. Logan asked me if I had any dreams. You've heard me go on often enough about how I'd like to teach languages like Mr. Topham at Haberdashers. I'd hardly got to the end of my sentence when, blow me down, Ellen pipes up that teaching's what she wants to do, too.

I didn't see anything wrong until her dad started to laugh. You should have seen Ellen's face; it sort of fell in on itself. When she tried to explain about how she wanted to go to university, her dad just blew his top and he told her that she would leave school next year on her fifteenth birthday to do war work. She just bolted from the table. I know what it feels like to have someone decide you should have no say in what you do. So I went after her.

It would have broken your heart. Ellen was standing on their back porch, no coat on, shivering, snowflakes landing on her. She was crying, too, but making no noise.

"Ellen," I said, "Come in. You'll catch your death out here."

She just shook hear head and she started to sob then, big, noisy gulping sobs that sounded like they hurt to come out. I didn't know what to do, so I started to talk. At first, it was just nonsense. You know, the things you say when you are trying to calm someone down. I got her to sit on this old bench, I found an old blanket that I think belonged to the dog — it was certainly smelly enough — and I put that around her shoulders. I told her about Dad and the blow-up we had when I told him I wasn't going back to school after my school certificate because I'd joined the RAF.

Ellen didn't stop crying, but I knew she was listening. I told her how I stood my ground, even when Dad said, "You'll end up on the gallows! They're all scum, are soldiers, even if you dress them in fancy uniforms and call them airmen!"

"Why?" she asked me, "Why does he feel like that?"

I felt a bit of a fool when I had to tell her that Dad won't ever talk about what happened to him in the Great War. But, I thought, that's better, if I can only keep Ellen talking, then maybe she'll calm down. The more I tried to explain, the more questions Ellen asked and then when I turned the tables on her, it all poured out: how she dreams of going to university, to study English or History.

People say that a person's face can light up, but I'd never seen it till then. Ellen told me about how she wanted to make people feel like she did about books, about how a book can take you any place in the world or in time. I knew just what she meant. She smiled and it made me want to smile, too.

We must have talked for about half an hour — my hands were almost the same blue as my uniform. Then Ellen's smile disappeared.

"He won't budge, you know, Stephen." Her voice was all dull then. "Dad didn't speak to Graham for almost a year after he spent his savings on flying lessons."

Just then, Colin stuck his head out the door and said, "Dad says you two are to come in, before you catch a chill."

Ellen just shrugged off the blanket. When we went in, all the dinner stuff had been cleared away. Mr. and Mrs. Logan were sitting in their armchairs in front of the fire. It all looked so normal.

"There you are," Mr. Logan said. "Did you young people have a good chat?"

Well, I didn't know what to make of that, but Ellen squared her shoulders and said, "Yes, Dad," all meek and mild.

"That's good," he said. Then he added, "It's getting late and more snow's forecast, so you'd probably better start back, Stephen. If you're lucky, you might be able to catch a ride."

I felt like I was being dismissed and I worried

that he might start in on Ellen again, but he just said, "I'm heading down to the Legion, so I can walk part of the way with you."

And that's what he did, chatting away like nothing had happened. Only there was one thing that was a bit odd. As we said goodnight, Mr. Logan said, "I'm sure your parents are very proud of what you're doing, young Stephen, and you'll be a good influence on my Ellen."

It has all left me feeling awkward. I'm not sure that I am going to be a good influence, and I'm not sure what to do. I've enjoyed visiting the Logans, but I can't abide arguments, and I don't want to provoke them. I do feel badly for poor Ellen. Her friends seem all right, if a bit flighty. I'd be willing to bet she's not told them about what she wants to do. You're the sensible one, Dorrie. Give me some advice, just like when I had the row with our dad. You know, that's given me an idea. I'm going to write to the Old Man, see if I can't break the ice. Don't say anything to him. Let it be a surprise. If he's caught off guard, he might just read it.

Your loving son and brother,
Stephen

★　　★　　★

1445326 LAC S. Dearborn
SFTS 16
Hagersville
Ontario
Canada

1st of December, 1942

Dear Dad,

I am hoping that you will read this and not just throw it away without even opening it. I am sure you know that I write regularly to Mum and Dorrie, and they to me, even though you don't like them to mention me.

I am in Canada now, completing my training. Come spring, all things being equal, I should be back in England with a squadron doing my bit. I will have some leave just before that happens and I would dearly like to spend it at home.

I've had a lot of time to think, Dad, and I'm beginning to understand why you were so angry about my decision to leave school. You said I was too young, and you were probably right. I felt helpless seeing others go off to fight, and I knew I had to do something, too. Waiting another two years, like you wanted me to, seemed like I was shirking, letting others do what I could be doing as well.

You were very proud of me when I won the scholarship to Haberdasher Aske's school and told me how important it was that I get a good education and make something of myself. I will still do that, and I am doing it even now. I have learned so much, Dad, about the world and about myself. You were right when you said I was too young. I *was* too young to make a decision like that, and I made it for some wrongheaded reasons. Flying isn't as glorious and exciting as I thought it would be, but I can do it, and I'm surprisingly good at it. Even my instructors say so! It's hard to say this, but if I don't make it through the war I hope my skills will have played a small part in defeating the Germans and making the world safe again. When faced with such an awful threat, we all have to put off our dreams and aspirations. You know that, Dad. If it hadn't been for the war you would have been retired by now, looking after your roses, not working extra shifts and doing duty as an air raid warden as well. It's the same for me. I have to do this now, and when it's all over I promise you that I'll make you proud again and complete my education.

If you've found it in your heart to read this letter, I am hoping that you'll reply. That will make things easier on Mum and Dorrie. They find it hard being caught in the middle like this.

Your respectful and loving son,
Stephen

CHAPTER

SEVEN

Sunlight glistened off the banked snow. Ellen stared at it until her eyes hurt, and then she squinched them tightly shut to watch the explosions of bright color behind her eyelids. She could hear Miss Arnott droning on about *The Merchant of Venice*, but Ellen let the words wash over her, trying to blur them into a meaningless hum as if a stray bee were loose in the cold classroom. Everyone said she was one of Arnie's pets, so she was in no danger of getting into trouble for her daydreaming. The worst that could happen would be a pat on the shoulder from Miss Arnott, and an understanding smile when the lesson ended. That was what had happened yesterday. When she had asked, "Still no news of Stewart, Ellen?" and Ellen had just nodded, Miss Arnott had been gentle. "The uncertainty must be the worst for you and your family, dear. I can understand it must be hard to keep your mind on your work, but do try. I have such high hopes of you, Ellen."

Ellen had felt a sharp stab of guilt. She hadn't been thinking of Stewart at all. Her mind had been endlessly replaying her father's stinging words after she had been foolish enough to confess her dream of becoming a teacher. What use were Miss Arnott's "high hopes?"

Ellen squeezed her eyelids together until they began to ache. When she opened them again, everything had become fuzzy. She didn't want to think about that argument again. A day or two following, when her father had been almost jolly, teasing her mother about her stunning way with leftovers, Ellen had tried to raise the subject of staying on at school. Her voice had been shaking and she braced herself for another explosion, but her father had sat very still, his face closed, his eyes unreadable. Without looking once at Ellen, he had quietly said, "That discussion is over, Ellen. Neither of us has any more to say on the matter."

So, here she was, stuck in lessons that no longer had any meaning. What was the bloody point?

A sharp elbow jolted into Ellen's side. She shook her head, thinking for one awful moment that she had spoken her last thoughts aloud.

"Stop it!" Barb hissed.

"Stop what?" Ellen was genuinely confused.

"Making faces, idiot." Barb's whisper was pitched low as she leaned toward Ellen. Inside the classroom, there was a general hum as people pulled out their scribblers and pencils. Miss Arnott had obviously given some instructions that Ellen had missed. Well, she'd get them from someone later.

"You've been doing it for the last ten minutes, and it makes you look dopey." Barb scrunched her face up, closing her eyes tightly. Ellen was sure, however, that she had not been sticking her tongue out of the side of her mouth like that. The effect was so ridiculous that Ellen couldn't help giggling.

"That's better! You've been a real misery lately, Ellen Logan." Barb's grin was infectious and Ellen found herself smiling back.

Ellen rocked back so her chair rested against the desk behind her, ignoring the tweak that its occupant gave her hair. "I was just playing a game Stewart and I used to do. If you close your eyes really tightly, you can see the most amazing colors."

"Yeah, but," Barb's puzzlement was evident in her voice, "why now? You're in English, Ellen. Your favorite subject, remember?"

Ellen shrugged.

"You're doing it again!" Ellen could hear real anger in her friend's voice. Miss Arnott looked in their direction. With a flick of her eyes, Ellen directed Barb's attention to the teacher. It worked. When Barb spoke again, she whispered. "You've been really odd lately, Ellen. You're miserable and moody, you daydream at school and if Deanna or I ask what's wrong, you clam up."

Ellen knew Barb was right, but she just couldn't tell them what was bothering her. Barb couldn't wait to leave school. She had it all planned: she would get a job as an office junior, work her way up to clerk and then get married and have babies. "Lots of them," she always added. Deanna was just hoping that the war wouldn't end before she was eighteen, old enough to join the Canadian Women's Royal Army Corps.

Stephen was the only person who understood. She smiled as she pictured him, shivering and blue with cold on the porch, trying desperately to stop her flood of tears, talking nonstop. It gave her hope — a little, anyway. Stephen was doing what he wanted, even though his father had not spoken to him since he left for training.

"Well?" Barb's fingers were tapping her desktop impatiently.

"It's nothing, Barb, really." Ellen flinched inside to hear herself sound so casually dismissive. "Well, the usual. No news of Stewart, Robbie's visit, Dad overworking and Mum out on committees every hour God sends." Ellen stopped and looked anxiously at her friend. "I did tell you about Robbie's visit, didn't I?" She relaxed when her friend nodded. "It just seems ..." Ellen tried to find the right words, saying them in her head before speaking. "It just seems as if I'm the only one doing nothing for the war effort." Paraphrasing her father's words, Ellen watched Barb's face closely, trying to gauge her friend's reaction. Her father had been so vehement. Maybe Ellen *was* being selfish.

"That's rubbish!" Barb's face was pink with indignation. "You're the one holding the family together, Ellen. If it wasn't for you, your mum couldn't be involved in half the stuff she is. And Colin would be even more of a brat than he is. You do know, don't you, that he tried to get Jeff to filch Mum's best eiderdowns for the camp they've made?"

Ellen grinned ruefully. "No, I didn't. I suppose Jeff got a good telling off for that."

"You'd better believe it. He'd got them halfway across the yard, trailing them through the snow, when Mum caught him. She was about to go storming over to your house to tell your mum what Colin had been up to. But then she figured your family's got enough to deal with."

"Phew! What a relief," Ellen said, knowing full well that she would probably have got the biggest telling off for not keeping a better eye on her brother.

"Hhhmmm! Hhhmmm!" Miss Arnott had crept up behind Barb and Ellen. Those heavy rubber-soled shoes could be surprisingly quiet. "So far you girls have not done a scrap of work. I never thought that I would have to be speaking to you like this, Ellen." With one chalk-covered finger she flipped through the text until she found what she was looking for. "Here. Now get to work immediately, looking for apt quotations for your essays." Her voice was sharper than Ellen had experienced. She added, "My patience has just about run out."

Ellen twisted uneasily in her seat. Miss Arnott's words had been harsh, but her eyes had been sad. Picking up her pencil, Ellen realized with dawning horror that she still didn't know what the essay's title was to be.

"Barb — " she started to whisper, but Miss Arnott, puce cardigan flapping, started back down the aisle toward them, her lips pursed with displeasure.

"Ellen Logan! What did I just say to you? Stand up!"

Ellen sprang to her feet, conscious of the shocked, disbelieving stares of her classmates. She heard a giggle, too, and was willing to bet it was Patsy Grant.

"I'm sorry, Miss Arnott. I was just going to ask Barb a question about the essay ..." Ellen stuttered to a halt. The principal's looming figure had come through the door and he was staring directly at Ellen.

"I'm very sorry to interrupt your class, Miss Arnott, particularly as it looks as if you have just called upon Miss Logan to speak." Mr. Hughes hesitated, almost as if he were unsure of what to say next. "I'm afraid that Ellen must come with me to my office. Her parents are waiting to speak to her."

The bones in Ellen's legs felt as if they had liquefied and she feared they would give way as she struggled to where Mr. Hughes waited. She tried to read his face — was that sorrow she saw in his eyes?

When she reached him, Mr. Hughes put his arm around her shoulders and firmly guided Ellen out of the door.

A gray mist was creeping up on Ellen, shrinking her vision to a narrow tunnel. She was conscious of her heart pounding, so loud that she was sure that Mr. Hughes must hear it. Placing one foot in front of the other, Ellen faltered when she heard Miss Arnott's wavery soprano struggling to make itself heard over the buzz of questions.

"Quiet down, class! Let us all pray that Ellen receives good news and, if not, let us make sure to offer her the support she will need."

✬   ✬   ✬

Ellen's feet flew over the hard-packed snow. Her boots were sturdy, but even so she had slipped a couple of times. It felt strange to be out after school, instead of at home preparing dinner. Her mother had insisted, though. "Getting dinner ready will give me something to do, Ellen," she had said. "It'll help keep my thoughts from whirling. Go and see Stephen if you need to, but don't stay long. It gets dark so early."

It was already nearly dark. Ellen shivered, pulling up her coat collar. She had no idea what to expect when she got to the camp. How was she going to see Stephen? Would she even be allowed to? Up ahead, the road was blocked by a barrier arm, and to one side of it there was a small building. Squaring her shoulders, Ellen increased her speed. Someone was bound to be in there, and they would either let her in or send for Stephen.

"Come to see your boyfriend, have you?"

The voice shocked Ellen. She looked frantically around trying to see who had spoken. She could make out a glowing point of light under a large tree, just off the road. As she moved closer, Ellen saw Patsy Grant and a couple of other girls passing around a cigarette. Although she didn't know their names, Ellen recognized the other girls. They had left high school the year she had started. They all looked pinched and cold. None of them were wearing boots or thick coats. Patsy was dressed like she was going to a dance. Ellen could have sworn her legs were bare. Her feet, jammed into high-heeled pumps, were mottled red and blue.

"Why are you here?" Ellen blurted out the question before she stopped to think.

The girls giggled, staring at her.

"Same reason as you, I guess." One of the girls sauntered over and walked round Ellen, sizing her up. "I don't think she's going to give us much competition, do you, girls?" she shouted back to the others. "She's dressed like a kid!"

Patsy came over. "It's the quiet ones you have to watch, Pauline. She may look like little Miss Goody-Two-shoes, but Ellen has snagged herself a pilot — one of the English boys, too."

Gritting her teeth, Ellen said, "How many times do I have to tell you, Patsy Grant, that he is *not* my boyfriend! He's a friend of the family. I've come to tell him news about Stewart, okay?"

The smile fell from Patsy's face. "Oh, yeah, Stewart. I forgot. Sorry." As Ellen stared openmouthed at her, Patsy continued. "Look, see that building there? That's the guardhouse. Tell them why you're here, and if one of them's in a good mood, he might get your guy over here. They'll believe you all right. Not like us — we've tried everything." She started to head back to the shelter of the tree, then put a hand toward Ellen. "I'm sorry about your brother. He was always nice to us when we were kids."

Ellen forced herself to breathe deeply. She had been all right until then, keeping her thoughts in check. Tears threatened to overwhelm her, but she gulped them down and went to the guardhouse.

The door was divided horizontally, and the top half was open. Ellen peered in and saw two men bundled in RCAF greatcoats. One was sitting in front of an oil radiator, desperately trying to warm his fingers, and the other was moving toward the door as he shrugged a rifle into place on his shoulder. He looked at Ellen and grinned before turning back to his companion. "Got another one here, Joe."

Ellen bristled slightly at his tone, and the way his eyes flicked over her. "Excuse me," she said. "I need to speak with LAC Stephen Dearborn, if that's possible." She could feel tears starting up in her eyes again. "I have some news for him."

"That sounds ominous," said the one by the fire, laughing. He stopped suddenly when he saw Ellen's mouth quiver. "I'm just kidding, sweetheart." Looking at the other man, he continued, "Dearborn's that quiet little English guy, over in H-block Two. Never had a girl ask for him before. What do you say we try and get him on the blower and get him over here?" Seeing Ellen's face brighten, he added, "I'm not promising anything. Ground school's over for the day, and if he's not in his H-block he could be anywhere, and I have no means of tracking him down."

"I'd be grateful if you could try," Ellen said. "It's really important."

The man who was standing winked at her. "They all say that," he said, before heading out the door.

Ellen watched him walk up and down just inside the barrier arm. She didn't understand quite what they were getting at — they seemed to find her coming here funny. She looked out again and saw Patsy and her friends leaning on the arm, talking to the guard as he patrolled up and down. She struggled to hear what they were saying, but only fragments of banter drifted up to her.

"You're in luck!" The airman in the hut put the receiver back on the hook with a thunk. "Dearborn was on his way to the mess hall, but one of his friends got a hold of him. He'll be here in a few minutes. Why don't you come in and warm yourself up by the fire till he gets here?"

"No, no, thank you. I'll be fine." Ellen neither liked nor understood the look of sympathy the guard was giving her. "I'll wait outside."

"Suit yourself." The airman picked up his pen and started making entries in a large ledger.

"Is he coming?" Patsy's raucous cry battered Ellen as soon as she set foot out of the door.

Not trusting herself to speak, Ellen nodded and then turned her back on the group by the barrier. She stared into the camp. A straight road ran away from the guardhouse. In the distance, she could see large, brightly lit buildings. Tinny music from a record player was carried on the wind, and Ellen tried to recognize the tune. She smiled. It was one of her favorites, "A Nightingale Sang in Berkeley Square."

A compact figure was hurrying toward her, muffled up in a greatcoat. Flying boots, still undone, flapped loosely as he trotted along the road. His cap was jammed on his head so hard that only his nose and eyes were visible. As he drew closer, Ellen could see that he looked anxious.

"Ellen?" Stephen grabbed hold of her arms. "What's wrong? What's happened?"

Ellen didn't have a chance to reply. Patsy's friends started to catcall and whistle. "Kiss her! That's no way to greet your girlfriend."

Stephen shot them a baleful glare and started to guide Ellen toward a building set a little way down the road from the guardhouse. "C'mon, Ellen, we can go into the Hostess House. I'll buy you a milk shake, and you can tell me what this is all about."

Pulling away from him, Ellen asked, "Are there people there?"

"Yes, of course. It's where we can entertain guests. There's a canteen and some sitting rooms, but it's never crowded, and," Stephen added, rubbing his ungloved hands, "it's a darn sight warmer than here."

"No!" Ellen felt herself losing control. She was aware of Patsy and the others openly listening to her and Stephen.

Stephen looked confused. "Well, where do you want to go? It's too late for me to go back home with you. I'm night flying later on."

Casting a glance at their audience, Ellen reached up and whispered in Stephen's ear, "Can you get out for about half an hour? We can go to Colin's camp. It's just round the corner, but I don't want them to know."

"Yes, whatever you want." Stephen yelled over to the airman in the guardhouse. "I'm just going to walk this young lady partway home." He took Ellen's arm, firmly tucked it in his and set off down the road, ignoring the whistles and kissing noises that followed them.

Ellen refused to answer any questions until they reached the camp, even though she could sense Stephen's anxiety. When tears started to trickle down her face, he silently handed her his handkerchief.

The camp was in a small hollow, just outside the perimeter fence. The boys had piled up branches and then stretched old blankets over them. Under the makeshift canopy were some rickety chairs and one armchair, whose left arm hung half off with trails of stuffing and horsehair bleeding from it.

"Sit yourself down," Stephen said, guiding Ellen into the armchair, "and tell me what this is all about." It was as if he suddenly noticed how white Ellen's face was. "You've had another row with your dad. Is that it, Ellen?" He hunkered down in front of Ellen, looking up at her. "Don't tell me you've done something daft like running away. You've got to go back, Ellen. This won't solve anything."

He's always the same, Ellen thought, when he's nervous or upset, Stephen talks. She smiled through her tears. "No, it's Stewart," she said simply. "He's alive."

"Blimey!" Stephen said, losing his balance and sitting with a thump. "Then why the bloody hell are you crying?" He picked himself up, brushing the snow from his coat. "Oh, you didn't half give me a turn, I can tell you. I thought it was bad news for sure."

"I can't help it." Ellen tried to knuckle the tears away. "Ever since we heard this morning, Mum and I can't stop laughing and crying. Sometimes, we do both at the same time." She shrugged. "Dad's the only one who's been calm about it."

"Oh, Ellen! That's wonderful news." Stephen hugged her tight, and then, as if realizing what he was doing, sprang away from her. "I've got a thousand questions, so why don't you just tell me what happened and what you heard." He pulled one of the rickety chairs over and carefully set it with its back facing Ellen. She smiled as he straddled it, just like Lowther had, and tipped back his hat in an almost perfect copy of Lowther's insouciance.

"A representative of the regiment phoned Dad at work. They had just had word that Stewart was being transferred to a prisoner-of-war camp in Germany."

Stephen couldn't contain himself. "But where's he been all this time? On the run and only just been captured?" He smiled at her. "You said he was a resourceful chap."

Ellen's face became solemn. "No, I wish it was that, Stephen. He was wounded, badly, we think, in the raid. The regiment's reading between the lines, but it seems like the Germans thought he wasn't going to make it, so instead of sending him to a military hospital, they left him at a convent so the nuns could take care of him … till he died." Ellen stifled a sob. "Do you think he'll be like Robbie?"

"I don't know, Ellen, honestly." Stephen looked stricken. He tried a smile. "But he must be okay if they're transferring him now."

"We don't know, Stephen. All we know is the camp. We don't know what shape he's in." Ellen put her head in her hands.

After gently prising her fingers apart, Stephen tilted Ellen's chin until she was forced to look at him. "You can write to him, Ellen, and he can write back. It'll take time, but you'll get your answers, I promise. Now, just be thankful he's alive!"

"Oh, Stephen, thank you!" Ellen twisted from Stephen's grasp and stood up. "You're right! In all the fuss today, it didn't occur to any of us that we can write to him."

Blushing, Stephen stood, too. "Don't thank me, Ellen. You or your parents would have realized that once you'd calmed down." He looked down at his boots. "I'm glad that you thought to come and tell me, though."

"Oh, Stephen! I'm so happy," Ellen stood on tiptoes and twirled round, her arms wide out. "Last one to the road is a rotten egg!" With that, she ran.

Stephen lumbered after her, his boots making him lurch and stumble. When he reached the road, Ellen was waiting, her cheeks pink with exertion, her eyes shining.

"Can you come and see us this weekend?" Ellen asked. "We're going to celebrate. A friend of Dad's has got a goose he's going to let us have." When Stephen looked doubtful, Ellen grabbed his hand. "Oh, do say you can, Stephen. Mum and Dad told me to ask you, so you needn't think you'd be intruding or anything stupid like that!" Sensing that he was still hesitating, Ellen added, "And I want you to come, too."

Impulsively, Stephen pecked her gently on the cheek.

She dropped his hand like a hot potato, and touched her cheek. "Why ever did you do that, Stephen Dearborn?" she asked, before she turned and ran down the road toward town.

EIGHT

1445326 LAC S. Dearborn
SFTS 16
Hagersville
Ontario
Canada

21st of December, 1942

Dear All,

You don't know how happy it makes me to start my letter like that. Your letter arrived a week ago, Dad, and I much appreciated it. As I said, I will make you proud of me. I promise.

So, what kind of Christmas will you have? With the bombing not so bad now, let's hope it's a quieter one! I'll be thinking of you a lot. This is my first Christmas away from home. There's going to be a whole parcel of things going on here, but it's not going to be the same. They've put up a huge tree in the mess hall; I couldn't believe it when I first saw it, and it's all covered with tinsel and angel hair. Makes our little tree in the back parlour look like a splinter, I can tell you. I was thinking of how we always waited until Christmas Eve to decorate the tree, and remembering how excited young Andrew got last year when we let him help for the first time, and how he wanted to go to bed really early because he couldn't wait for Father Christmas to come. I've sent a couple of parcels home, some goodies I don't think you can get easily, presents for all of you and a special one for Andrew, just so he doesn't forget his Uncle Stephen. As well as a toy, I've put in my old flying helmet since I've got a new one. It's a bit battered, but I hope he'll like it. All the kids round here are desperate for things like that, so Lowther, the New Zealander I told you about, he gave me his old one for Ellen's young brother, Colin. Ellen told me Colin was so pleased with it that he even wore it to bed. He must have looked a right sight!

I can't believe it. I've written a page and I haven't told you the really important news. Ellen's brother Stewart is alive. They finally got word that he'd been wounded and was only just being transferred to a POW camp. There was a lot of confusion, apparently, because he hadn't been in a military hospital. You can imagine how happy the Logans are, although they're still worried because they don't know how badly he was wounded and whether he's going to be permanently crippled. Ellen's been writing to him every day, but she hasn't had any reply back yet. She was a bit glum about that, but I told her how long our letters can take and, if you add in the fact that Jerry isn't going to make POWs' mail a top priority, then she can't expect too much.

You've probably gathered that I've been visiting the Logans quite a bit. What with the bad weather restricting our flying time, there's been a lot more time when I can get away from the base. The row between Ellen and her dad seems to have worked itself out, or so it seems to me. She tells me that he hasn't said a word about her leaving school next year. So, I think it was something and nothing, just angry words spoken in the heat of the moment. Mr. Logan can be a bit stern, but he loves his family and he'll do what's best for them.

In a funny sort of way, I can't say that I'm sad the row happened, because I learned a lot about Ellen that I might never have known otherwise. I've never met anyone who is so passionate about books. She likes the same ones I do, and it's such a relief to be able to talk about them, and about poetry, without people thinking I'm a sissy. Do you remember that poem I liked so much that starts: "If I should die, think only this of me: / That there's some corner of a foreign field / That is forever England." Well, it's one of Ellen's favourites, too!

And she's bright. She sees things in a poem that I don't, so I've learned a lot from her. We exchange books, too, and that does help to pass the time, although the other chaps sometimes give me a bit of stick about always having my nose in a book. Some of them have started calling me the Prof. It beats Swee'Pea, I suppose, and you never know, one day I might just be a professor. How does that sound, Professor Stephen Dearborn? Very grand, eh?

We had our carol service here yesterday, and it made me feel very homesick. They sang my favourite, "Oh Come, Oh Come, Emmanuel," and I got a bit choked up when it came to the line, "… that into exile drear has gone …", because that's how I've been feeling a bit, but not so much now. There's a party here tomorrow afternoon for the airmen who have families nearby. Lowther's volunteered to dress up as Father Christmas, or Santa Claus, as they call him here. He's going to have a fake beard, but he's brushing his moustache with talcum powder to make it white. He'll be a hoot. There's also a dance on Christmas Eve, but I don't think I'll go. You know me, two left feet and I never know what to say to girls.

On Christmas Day, I'm going to be spoiled with not one, but two Christmas dinners. We have a parade at 10:15 in the morning and then Christmas dinner will be served to us by the officers, no less. After that, our time is our own, so Mrs. Logan has invited me to join them for their

Christmas dinner in the late afternoon. I didn't know whether it was the right thing to do, but I got them some small gifts. Some tobacco for Mr. Logan, handkerchiefs for Mrs. Logan, a toy plane for Colin that one of the lads here made and a book for Ellen of Robert Browning's poems. Do you think they'll think I'm being a bit presumptuous? That's daft — I don't know why I'm asking you, because Christmas will likely have come and gone before you get this letter and reply! I'll just give them the gifts and hope for the best.

It's later in the afternoon now. I stopped writing as we had ground school. The mail had arrived when I got back to barracks, including your letter, Dorrie, telling me about Alan. Give my sympathies to his parents when you see them. I think I'll close this letter now.

Your loving son and brother,
Stephen

✫ ✫ ✫

The huge wind was terrifying. It howled past the fuselage of the plane, battering Stephen's ears and taking his breath away.

His face felt strange, too, as if it had been frozen, and now the skin at his temples and around his eyes was stretching tight. He had a desperate urge to go to the toilet; his bowels roiled and rumbled. Gritting his teeth, Stephen prayed that he could control his stomach. The other chaps would never let him live it down if he messed himself like a baby. Already they called him Swee'Pea after Popeye's baby, because he was the youngest on the course. His terror lifted and he smiled quickly; they would be amazed if they knew just how young he was. He shook himself as great waves of fear swept through him again. "Stupid!" he tried to yell, although his mouth didn't seem to be working properly. "You're in a spiral dive." The wind, the tightness in his face, all made horrible sense. It was textbook, just like Warrant Officer Mackay had described to them back in the classroom.

Frantically, Stephen tried to remember what to do. He looked despairingly over his shoulder — maybe one of the other chaps would know. It was so odd, he thought. They should have been yelling at him by now, banging his shoulders. Lowther would normally have been grabbing at the stick, calling him a bloody idiot! Where were they all? He thought of Mackay again, tried to remember what he had told them to do. Stephen's mind was blank. He kept seeing Mackay's face, seeing his gingery handlebar mustache twitch as he smiled and said, "Ah, but none of my laddies are going to be fool enough to get themselves into a dive, are they?"

All the switches and dials in front of him meant nothing. Stephen looked down at his hands, clumsy in leather gauntlets, clutching the stick. Tentatively, he lifted one, watched how slowly it moved. The air had solidified and it took all his strength to push through it. He pulled hard back. Nothing happened.

The wind was getting louder. There was a metallic screaming that hurt Stephen's ears. At first he thought the plane was breaking apart, then he realized that he was making the noise, a high-pitched, keening wail that tore his throat. Through the windscreen of the cockpit, he could no longer see sky, just the brown and green blur of the ground that was hurtling toward him. Instinctively, Stephen threw his hands in front of his face, knowing, even as he did it, that it was useless. Nothing could save him now.

With a shudder, Stephen jolted awake and lay unmoving, staring up at the bottom of Lowther's bunk, watching the thin mattress bulge and then flatten out as Lowther squirmed to get comfortable. His heart was racing and, despite the frigid air in the barrack room, he was sweating, so much that his flannel pajamas were sodden. He held his hand in front of his face, half surprised to see that it was ungloved. The nightmare was back again. He hadn't had it for a while, but now it was back in all its sweaty, gut-churning glory.

Stephen shuddered and turned over so that he faced the wall. He closed his eyes, knowing that he wouldn't sleep. He tried to picture Alan's face, but he couldn't see it clearly in his mind. All he could conjure up was the tank that had featured so prominently in the photo that Alan had sent with his last letter. In it, Alan had been tanned and lean, grinning as he leaned against the tank's huge bulk, one arm resting on it like you might put your arm around a girl's shoulders. The tank had been newly painted in desert camouflage. Now Stephen saw it as a skeleton, a wreck, its paint blistered and leprous, its tracks blown off by the mine that had killed it and, sticking out from its turret, a burned claw of a hand.

☆　　☆　　☆

1445326 LAC S. Dearborn
SFTS 16
Hagersville
Ontario
Canada

22nd of December, 1942

Dear Dorrie,

    I am writing this letter just to you, knowing that you are the only one who ever picks up the post. I'm sorry my last letter ended so abruptly. The news about Alan knocked me for six. He and I have been friends since we started at Gellately Road School together when we were just five. We were the "clever" boys of the class, and everyone had such hopes for us.

    It's funny, but most of the time you never think about anything like that happening, especially not to you or someone you know. It's always going to be the other bloke who gets the chop. When you do think of it, it's awful because that's all you can think about. Everything you're doing seems dangerous and frightening and you have to force yourself to do stuff that was just routine before. Funk, getting in a funk, that's what the chaps here call it, not that we talk about it much, but it happens. For most of us, it passes. You've just got to find something to take your mind off it. I'm hoping Christmas will do the trick for me. No, there's no hoping about it — it will, I know. Here am I sounding all gloomy, Dorrie, and you don't need to hear that. It's not the reason I was writing just to you, anyway.

I need your advice, Dorrie. After all, what's a big sister for? I'm hoping this letter will reach you and your reply will get back to me in time. You know that dance I mentioned, the one on Christmas Eve? Well, I lied about it. I did want to go, but I couldn't bring myself to. I wanted to take Ellen, see, but I didn't have the nerve to ask her. It's all too late now, but there's going to be a big New Year's Eve dance, and I was thinking that I might ask her to that. What do you think? Should I?

I know Ellen's just fourteen, but when we talk it's like we're the same age, Dorrie. I've never met anyone like her, anyone I feel so comfortable with. When I'm with her, I don't gabble like I do with people who make me nervous ... well, not anymore. I used to when I first met her family, and I think I used to get on her nerves because I don't think she liked me very much to start with. Do you think she's too young? I know you were only just fifteen when you met Ron, and you were married when you were sixteen. Don't get the wrong idea or anything — I don't want to marry Ellen or anything like that. All I want is to take her out by myself, not visit her as a family friend. I think her parents would let her come. They seem to really like me. Mr. Logan said I'm a "steady lad," so I'm sure they'd trust me to take good care of her. We could even go as part of a group, if that made them feel happier. Evans, one of the other chaps, has been keen on one of Ellen's friends ever since he saw her at the church bazaar, and he keeps finding excuses to come to town with me in the hope of seeing Barb again. He'd jump at a shot to take her out.

You'd really like Ellen, Dorrie. She's not what you'd call pretty-pretty, but she's got a lovely smile. She's not small, maybe about five foot, four inches, a couple of inches shorter than me — phew! She's got sandy hair, like her dad, and blue eyes. She complains about her hair, because she says it's wiry and hard to manage, but it looks okay to me. I'm rambling on. I have a photograph of the two of us at her parents' house, so I'll send that and then you can picture Ellen when I talk about her. It doesn't do her justice, though, not really, because you can't hear her talk and that's what I like most about her: she talks, she doesn't chatter just for the sake of it. She thinks about things and you can talk about ideas with her. She's got a bit of a temper, too, but I haven't been on the receiving end of it, thank goodness. I've seen her when she got cross with her brother, Colin, not that it bothered him. Sometimes, when we're together, we just sit and read, neither of us saying a word, just happy in each other's company.

You're the only person I can ask for advice,

Dorrie. I couldn't ask any of the other chaps. Well, maybe I could ask Lowther. He's got a serious side that he works hard at hiding. No, it wouldn't be on, because I'd be letting on that I've never asked a girl out before, and that might raise a few questions I don't want to have to answer. So, Dorrie, dear, I'm counting on you to come up with the goods. And if you think I should, a few tips on how to treat a girl when you take her out for the first time wouldn't go amiss.

Your loving and not-so-little brother,
Stephen

P.S. Has Graham Logan been in contact with you yet? His last letter said that he had been posted nearer to you and was going to try and get in touch, maybe set up a visit on his next 48-hour pass.

NINE

The dress had been hanging on the front of the wardrobe ever since her aunt had brought it over on her post-Christmas visit. Ellen and her mother had started work on it immediately, shortening it and taking it in so that it fitted Ellen's more compact body. Her aunt had made it just before the war started and had only worn it once, to a dinner dance. Ellen stroked the raised embroidered pattern — lilac broderie anglaise — then traced the dress's sweetheart neckline, wondering whether it might reveal too much of her chest, and whether it was such a good idea in winter. She shook her head. It would be fine. Her father had said that he would use some of his gasoline ration to drive her and Barb to the camp. As long as they wrapped up in coats and scarves, they would be warm enough until they got to the Opera House. It sounded so grand, an opera house on a military camp, but Stephen had laughed at the look of awe on Ellen's face, saying it was just a big hall where all the camp's main social events were held — quizzes, films shows and dances.

Positioned directly under the dress stood the shoes that Ellen's aunt had given her to match. Heeled pumps in purple suede with peep-toes — the first high-heeled shoes Ellen had ever had. Ellen had felt wobbly and strange when she tried them on. She had worn them around the house to get used to them until Colin had started to tease her. He had been insufferable ever since Stephen had asked her to the New Year's Dance. Whenever he saw her, he would mutter:

Ellen and Stephen sitting in a tree,

K-I-S-S-I-N-G.

First comes love, then comes marriage,

Then comes Ellen with a baby carriage!

She had tried everything to get him to stop. She explained that she and Stephen were just friends and going to a dance was just something fun to do, like going to a friend's birthday party would be. When that didn't work she had yelled at him, and even chased him about the house until she caught him and clipped him round the ear. Colin had gone running to her mother, crying loudly, but he still managed a smirk at Ellen, and Ellen had very nearly been banned from going. It was only the thought of disappointing Stephen that had made her mother relent.

Ellen flung herself down on her bed and lay on her back with her head on her hands, staring at the ceiling. She still found it difficult to believe that she was going. No one had ever asked her to a dance, and when

Stephen did, she had blurted out, "Why?"

Stephen had blushed and mumbled something, and Ellen had had to ask him to repeat himself. "I just thought it would be a laugh, that's all." Stephen had continued, "The other chaps have been on at me about never going to anything like that, so I thought if I asked you, it would get them off my back a bit."

"Oh," Ellen had said, surprised at the twinge of disappointment she felt, though she had no idea why.

"It was Evans's idea." Stephen had shrugged dismissively. "He really likes your friend Barb, and he wants to ask her. But he thought he'd have more chance of her saying yes if you were going, so that's why I'm asking you." Stephen was studying the floor very intently, which Ellen had found very strange.

"My parents probably won't let me, Stephen. Dad can be funny about stuff like that."

Stephen had thought for a moment, then had said, "Why don't I ask him, or maybe we can ask him together?"

That's what they did in the end. Ellen smiled as she remembered how Stephen had gone red and stumbled over the words. He had waited until just after dinner on Christmas Day, when Colin was safely up in his bedroom playing with the model plane Stephen had given him. Mr. Logan had leaned back in his chair, one large freckled hand clasping a tumbler of whisky, interrupting Stephen's tortuous explanation of how they would be part of a group with his friend, Roger Evans, and Ellen's friend, Barb. "Why not, Stephen, my laddie? Just so long as you take good care of her."

Both Ellen and Stephen had been stunned into silence.

"What's the matter with the pair of you, gawking at me like a pair of loons? Did you think I'd say, 'No?'" He'd cast a sly smile over at Ellen's mother, who'd been sipping a glass of port. "You're getting to be a big, bonnie lassie, Ellen. You put me in mind of your mother when I first saw her. And if her father hadn't let me walk out with her, despite the fact she was only a bit older than you, well you wouldn't be here now!"

It had been Ellen's turn to blush.

Ellen closed her eyes. She still couldn't believe that persuading him had been so easy. No, there hadn't even been any persuading. Levering herself off the bed, Ellen crossed to the window, rubbing her cold hands. She peered down the road, straining to see if Barb was on her way. Ellen's mother had suggested that the two girls get dressed together and she would help them with their hair. Barb had been so excited when Ellen told her that Stephen's friend thought she was cute and wanted to invite her to the dance, but she was sure her parents would object. Surprisingly, Ellen's father had come to the rescue. He knew Barb's father from the Legion and told him how they had got to know Stephen and what a nice lad he was, and how his friends would be the same. And, after all, these young men were far from home training to defeat the Nazis and deserved a little fun. It had worked, and here was Barb, a small suitcase in hand, struggling against the fierce wind.

Ellen ran down the stairs and was standing shivering in the doorway by the time Barb had opened the Logans' gate and was picking her way up the path, avoiding the icy patches.

"My, don't you look lovely?" Barb's expression was mischievous as she took in Ellen.

"But, I haven't even started getting ready," Ellen said. Barb's giggle and knowing look at her head made Ellen's hand fly up to the rags that her mother had curled her hair around. "Baaarb!" she said with mock indignation. Then with one hand on her hip, Ellen pirouetted, and in her most refined voice said, "Madam doesn't appreciate the latest style — practical and with the great advantage of keeping one's head warm while avoiding 'hat head,' the scourge of modern girls!"

"Ellen?" Mrs. Logan's voice was impatient. "If that's Barb, let her in and stop letting all the heat out."

"You heard your mother!" Barb said and sashayed past Ellen, unable to resist tweaking one of her rag curlers.

"Oooow!" Ellen yelped, slamming the door.

* * *

As the car reached the camp gates, Ellen peered out, wishing that she had chosen to sit in the front, instead of in the back with Barb. It would have been easier to see whether Stephen and Roger were waiting as they had promised.

"There they are! Is that them?" Barb leaned across

Ellen to point to two figures huddling in the shelter of the guardhouse.

The general shape was right: a small, stocky figure alongside a taller, more gangly one. "Yes, I think so. Dad, just stop here, and we'll get out." Ellen was fumbling with the door handle, when she said, "Thank you, Dad." She wanted to say more, but couldn't find the right words.

"Ah, you're welcome, lassie." Mr. Logan's voice was gruff. "You girls have a good time now, and make sure that those lads look after you. Otherwise, they'll have me to answer to." He looked out at Stephen and Roger, who were making their way toward the car. "I'll be back here at one o'clock to pick you up." He laughed. "Your mother wanted you back by midnight, but I told her that you needed to see the new year in properly, and I want to do the same myself with a wee dram before I come out again. Mind you, girls, staying out so late won't be happening again."

"We'll be here, Mr. Logan, and thanks," Barb said as she and Ellen bundled out of the car.

A blast of icy wind met them and Ellen shivered. With only the thin cotton dress underneath, her coat offered little protection.

"Well, ladies," Roger spoke first. "We were beginning to think you had stood us up. Stephen here was getting into a right flap," he said, playfully cuffing Stephen's head and knocking his cap off.

"Don't exaggerate, Evans. Let's get moving. It's freezing." Stephen picked up his cap and set off into the camp, leaving the others no choice but to follow him.

Ellen found it hard to match his pace, so she trailed a few steps behind him. She glared at his back and wondered why she had put so much effort into getting ready when Stephen had barely acknowledged her presence. To make matters worse, Roger was really turning the charm on Barb a little behind her. He had offered Barb his arm, just in case she might slip, and was talking a mile a minute. Barb kept giggling, and each giggle made Ellen's mood sour more.

The lights of the Opera House gilded the snow and hid the grime that passing feet had stamped into it. A Glenn Miller tune was drifting out. Ellen heard "American Patrol" and felt her spirits lift — she loved that sort of music and hoped that Stephen would dance to it with her. Her older brothers had an old gramophone, and whenever their friends had come over, out it would come and they would dance to swing music. Ellen used to sit in the doorway, hoping that one of them would notice her and invite her to join in. Once they realized how she loved to dance, and that being so small made her easy to practice the more complicated moves with, Ellen became a favorite. The boys had left her the gramophone and their records, and she, Barb and Deanna would get it out every so often, roll back her bedroom carpet and dance — but it wasn't the same.

"I'll show you where the cloakroom is, where you can leave your coats and change your shoes." Stephen's voice cut into Ellen's thoughts. He pointed at her sturdy boots. "I assume you're going to change. Otherwise, maybe I should get my flying boots for protection." He ducked his head and grinned, looking more like his usual self. "On second thought, perhaps you'd better keep the boots on, Ellen. I'll confess, I'm not much of a dancer."

Ellen patted the sleeve of Stephen's uniform. "As long as we get to dance, I don't mind." She grabbed Barb by the arm and headed into the cloakroom, which was a perfumed mass of girls, changing their shoes and touching up their makeup and hair.

With their coats and boots safely stored, Ellen was about to head for the hallway when Barb stopped her. She shouldered her way to a mirror and with an air of triumph brought out of her clutch bag a small pot of rouge, a block of mascara and a gleaming bullet-shaped tube of lipstick.

"Barb! Where on earth did you get this?" Ellen's admiration was evident in her voice.

"Deanna and friends. Everyone kicked in what they could. We don't want to look like pasty-faced schoolgirls, do we?" She held out the mascara to Ellen. "You go first with this."

Tentatively opening the case, Ellen picked up the tiny brush and remembered watching one of Graham's girlfriends. She spat delicately onto the hard black cake and worked the brush in it. It was hard to get the mascara on her eyelashes without clumping it, but she managed. The result was amazing. Her sandy, light eyelashes now looked dark and mysterious. She applied the lipstick carefully. Tangee Natural — a particularly repellent shade of tangerine in the tube, but the ads Ellen had seen in her mother's *Chatelaine* magazine claimed it would turn "lips a most becoming shade of blush rose." Ellen squinted into the mirror. Blush rose she wasn't sure about, but she did look different, that was for sure — older and with the clusters of sausage ringlets softly framing her face, almost, she dared to think, pretty.

Their hands in their pockets, Roger and Stephen leaned nonchalantly against the wall, brass buttons and buckles gleaming. She couldn't resist a smile. A wavy cowlick was escaping from the Brylcreem-smooth hair that Stephen had obviously worked hard on.

"My, oh my!" Roger was staring at Barb appreciatively. "Don't you look lovely!"

Ellen looked at her friend. Roger was right. With her small, heart-shaped face and fine blond hair, Barb had a natural prettiness; but tonight, in a navy dress printed with small sprigs of forget-me-nots, it was almost as if she had turned into the woman she would become.

Ellen was conscious of Stephen staring at her, but he just looked away guiltily when she met his gaze. Humph! Ellen tossed her head so her ringlets bounced. "Are we going to stay here all night, gawking at each other? Or are we actually going to dance?" Ellen sounded rude and ungracious, but she didn't care.

As they entered the dance, Ellen stopped in amazement. The dance floor, awash with colored lights, was filled with couples jitterbugging, the men's blue uniforms a backdrop for the bright colors of their partners' clothes. On a stage at the far end, a uniformed band was doing its best to imitate Glenn Miller's Army Air Force Band, with fair success. Arranged around the sides of the room were tables where couples sat watching. There was an air of hectic excitement in the air that made Ellen long to be part of it. She turned to Stephen, ready to drag him onto the floor, but he was standing on tiptoe and waving. In the far corner, Ellen saw an answering wave.

"C'mon, Ellen. Lowther said he'd save us a spot. Let's get over there, get settled, and then, I promise, I'll dance." He grinned. "I know that's the only reason you agreed to come. Your mum told me how mad you are about dancing!"

With Barb and Roger trailing behind them, Ellen and Stephen wormed their way through the tightly packed crowd to the table where Lowther lounged, a glass of beer in his hand. He raised it to them, as they flopped into the chairs. "Finally! I've been fighting off invaders for the last half hour. Let me get everyone a drink, then the fun can begin. What'll it be? Beer for the gentlemen and . . . for the ladies?" Lowther gave them an amused look, which turned into a wink when both Barb and Ellen asked for ginger ale.

Ellen could see that Barb was as awestruck as she was. As she stared around the room, Ellen started to recognize familiar faces: older girls who were friends of Stewart's and Graham's, and even Patsy Grant, dancing with the guard who had been on duty when Ellen had come to the camp. Patsy waved as she went past, winking and giving Stephen a thumbs-up.

"Well, Ellen, let's give it a whirl." Ellen took Stephen's hand and allowed him to lead her onto the dance floor. She was surprised how warm and dry his hand was. She had remembered it as being sweaty.

The band had started "Chattanooga Choo Choo," and Ellen tried to follow Stephen's lead, only to realize that he had not been joking about being a poor dancer. His face was getting red, and his steps were becoming more hesitant. "Relax, Stephen. Don't try to jitterbug. Let's do something simpler." Relieved, Stephen assumed a more traditional stance, one hand holding hers, the other resting on the small of her back. With only a minimum of subtle pushing, Ellen was able to steer Stephen around the floor without tripping or bumping into other couples. Glancing over his shoulder, Ellen saw that Roger could certainly dance, particularly the wilder movements that involved swinging his partner. Barb didn't seem to mind.

"There, that wasn't too bad. Ellen, you're a good teacher," Stephen said gratefully. "I've been terrified ever since I asked you that I was going to make a total idiot of myself. I've had the collywobbles about it all day, so I was probably really grumpy when you arrived. I'm sorry."

Disarmed, Ellen smiled. Although she watched wistfully as the other dancers did more than just shuffle around, she was soon giggling at the dry little remarks Stephen made about people. He had a keen eye and his observations were dead on. When he called Patsy Grant a limpet, so tightly was she holding on to her partner, he made Ellen laugh so much that she had to sit down. Lowther was waiting at the table, a line of empty glasses showing that he had been keeping busy. Both Ellen and Stephen reached for drinks, thirsty after their exertion. Ellen was surprised to see Stephen pull a face and almost splutter as he took his first sip of beer.

"You'll make a dancer out of Swee'Pea yet, Miss Logan!" Lowther said. "Indeed, the young sprog has positively blossomed since he met you."

Stephen was staring at the table, his face beet red. "Stephen's become like a member of our family," Ellen offered, hoping that Lowther would drop the subject.

"Oh, is that what you want to be, Swee'Pea, Ellen's big brother?" Lowther asked knowingly, watching Stephen's face closely.

Stephen's discomfort was growing and he had started to look almost angry. Quickly, Ellen spoke. "Mr. Lowther, did you not want to bring anyone to the dance?"

Lowther swung his head round, "George, Ellen, call me George. Mr. Lowther makes me feel very old. I'm already considered to be the Old Man of the group by these youngsters, so I don't need reminding of my vast age. Which is," he added with a half laugh, "twenty-five."

"I'm sorry, George," Ellen said, managing to use his name with only the slightest of hesitations. "I didn't mean to pry or to offend you." She felt as if she had been rebuked by a teacher.

"No, Ellen, you didn't." He ran a hand through his hair. "I've got the blues tonight. I've a wife and son back home, and I keep thinking about them. Not that I've ever seen the tyke, except in pictures. He was born six months after I left New Zealand. So, although I may talk like a ladies' man, that's all it is, talk. My Pat will be waiting for me when this bloody war is over."

Lowther smiled at Ellen. "Oh, Ellen, you've gone all serious on me, looking at me with those beautiful, big blue eyes. Swee'Pea would never forgive me if I made his girl sad." Before Ellen could protest that she was not Stephen's girl, Lowther stood up and with a courtly bow asked, "May I have the pleasure of this dance?"

After a quick glance at Stephen, who shrugged helplessly, Ellen took the hand that Lowther held out to her.

For fifteen minutes Ellen was whirled around the dance floor as she had never been before. Lowther didn't so much dance as glide, and it was easy to follow even his most complicated moves. At one point, laughing and almost out of breath, Ellen found herself shooting through Lowther's legs to come up grinning on the other side, as the couples around them clapped and cheered. Soon after, Stephen's face appeared over Lowther's shoulder. "Can I reclaim Ellen now?"

With another of his extravagant gestures, Lowther handed Ellen over and backed away through the crowd, blowing kisses at anyone and everyone.

"I'm a dreadful comedown after that," Stephen said ruefully, as he shuffled Ellen around the floor. "Sometimes I think Lowther's stark-raving bonkers."

"No," Ellen said with a certainty that surprised her, "he's not crazy, just a good actor. Underneath all the show and the jokes, he's lonely."

Stephen pushed Ellen away so that he could look into her face, his hand still resting on her shoulder. "That's what I like about you, Ellen, the way you think about people, how you can see what they're really feeling." For a moment he was lost in thought. When he did finally speak, it was hesitatingly. "Look, this is a bit of a cheek, especially since I asked you here to dance, but would you step outside with me for a minute, Ellen?"

Ellen was puzzled. Outside? It was so cold. Still, there was something in his eyes, an unspoken plea that made her agree. "Okay, just let me grab my coat."

As soon as they got outside, Ellen felt she had made a huge mistake. Propped up against the walls were couples in tight clinches, their mouths locked together for what seemed an impossibly long time. How did they breathe? she wondered. Surely this was not why Stephen had wanted to come here. He had taken her hand outside the cloakroom, and now he pulled her along until he found a deserted spot under a tree. There was small bench, and he cleared the snow from it.

Shivering, Ellen wrapped her coat tighter around herself. She felt tense and exposed, convinced that everyone was staring at them.

"Ellen," Stephen stopped, took a deep breath and continued, "Lowther got it wrong when he said I wanted to be your big brother. I may have to start with, but I don't anymore." He took Ellen's face between his hands and pulled her gently toward him. "I really like you," he said, his breath warm and smelling of beer against her cheeks. "I've never ever liked a girl the way I like you, but I don't want to make a fool of myself if you don't feel the same way about me."

Ellen felt as if she had fallen down an elevator shaft. Her thoughts were whirling so fast that she couldn't work out how she was feeling. Finally, she said the first thing that came into her head. "But you're too old for me, Stephen. I'm only fourteen."

Stephen threw back his head and howled with laughter, laughter so wild that it left him gasping. Wheezing, he eventually managed, "Ellen, how old do you think I am?"

"Twenty, twenty-one." Why was Stephen asking her such a daft question?

"Ellen," he said, his voice serious, "I've just had my seventeenth birthday, not that I celebrated it. I didn't dare in case anyone found out that I'd lied to join up. I told them all my papers had been destroyed in a bombing raid." Stephen leaned over and gently kissed Ellen's mouth.

TEN

1445326 LAC S. Dearborn
SFTS 16
Hagersville
Ontario
Canada

1st of January, 1943

Dear Dorrie,

I did it. I asked Ellen to the dance! I didn't wait for your letter, which was just as well, as it only arrived yesterday. I mustered up all my courage and asked her just before Christmas. Roger Evans helped. I told you that he's a bit sweet on one of Ellen's friends, and he kept going on at me about making up a foursome. I was convinced she'd turn me down flat, but it all worked out, and we didn't even have any trouble getting her dad to let her go. That surprised Ellen, I can tell you.

I don't understand girls, though, Dorrie. I think I know Ellen really well, but then she'll say or do something that really puzzles me. Like at the dance, one minute she was all grumpy, the next minute all smiles. I didn't do too badly with the actual dancing, but I'm a bit of a stick compared to some of the other chaps. You should have seen Lowther. He took Ellen off to dance, and it was like watching Fred Astaire with Ginger Rogers in the films. He made it all look so easy. It made me quite jealous, so I cut in after a while. Lowther's okay, though. He's been giving me some dancing lessons in the barracks, even though some of the others have been giving us a ribbing about it. He just smiles at them and says, "Got to teach the sprog some social skills!"

Oh, and one last thing, Dorrie. I told Ellen about liking her and all. It was just before her dad was coming to pick her and Barb up. I've no idea what she's going to make of it. I just hope I didn't come on too strong and scare her off. I really, really like her.

Your loving brother,
Stephen

★   ★   ★

1445326 LAC S. Dearborn
SFTS 16
Hagersville
Ontario
Canada

1st of January, 1943

Dear Mum, Dad and Dorrie,

First of all, a Happy New Year to you all! Can you believe it's 1943? The fourth year of war! Surely it can't go on much longer, but the news hasn't been good. I've been thinking of you all a lot today. Flying has been canceled for the last two days because of poor weather conditions, so time is hanging heavy for us all. I try to picture how you will be spending your day. Dad smoking his pipe and reading his newspaper. Mum lying on the couch in front of the fire with the dog next to her. I was sorry to hear that your arthritis has been so bad, Mum. Dorrie in the kitchen cooking, while Ron and Andrew play Ludo. I'll bet it was a nice surprise Ron getting leave, and I'm sure he was grateful for your cooking, Dorrie. I know I would be. Do you know what I miss most? Your jam roly-poly with custard. They feed us like kings and we don't lack for anything, but it's the homey things you miss. I'd give anything for some Fry's chocolate from Mrs. Green at the corner shop, but I suppose that's rationed, too!

There's rumours that we might get held back
and not graduate on time, because this rotten
weather has kept us from putting in enough
flying hours. I hope that's not true, because I've
had enough. I'm ready to get out there and face
the Jerries. I think we all are. Even when we
get back to England, we're still not going to be
operational straight away. We'll have to familiarize
ourselves with whatever planes we'll be flying. I'd
love to be a fighter pilot, but I have a feeling I'll
end up on a bomber squadron. All I pray is that I
don't get stuck here in Canada as an instructor.
We all dread that.

But I'm going to be sad to leave Canada in
a way. The Logans have been so kind to me,
treating me like a son. Mrs. Logan told me that
she'd had a letter from her Graham and that he
had visited you. He liked your cooking, too,
Dorrie! What did you think? He's a bit of a lad,
isn't he? Did he come alone or bring some of his
pals? His sister, Ellen, is the one I've got to know
best and I took her to the New Year's Eve dance
here last night. She's not like Graham, being
much quieter, but she looks like him, with sandy
hair and blue eyes. She's really very nice. Did you
get the photograph I sent yet? It's one her dad
took of the two of us in their back garden. We'd
just come back from walking their dog, just
before the really cold weather started. I'm going
to ask Ellen if she'll write to me when I ship out.

I think she will — well, I'm hoping she will.

News is scarce, really. I told you all about Christmas, and I don't want to repeat myself. Keep your chins up. Just think, maybe I'll be home in a couple of months.

Your loving son and brother,
Stephen

P.S. I'll also write to Alan's parents. I should imagine that Christmas has been difficult for them.

★　　★　　★

1445326 LAC S. Dearborn
SFTS 16
Hagersville
Ontario
Canada

1st of January, 1943

Dear Mr. and Mrs. Grainger,

Dorrie sent me the sad news about Alan. This must be a dreadful time for you and yours. I just wanted to tell you that Alan was the best friend anyone could have. All through our school years, he was an important part of my life. He always saw the funny side of things and that was good because, as I'm sure you remember, I can take things a bit too seriously. He was always loyal and kind.

I could tell you things like Alan gave his life for his country, but you know that already, and that probably isn't important now, although it may come to be later. What I can say is that Alan went willingly to fight. We both did. We may not have thought about the risks we were facing — at the beginning we thought it all a big adventure — but that changes. I just hope that I can be as brave as Alan was.

Yours sincerely,
Stephen Dearborn

ELEVEN

A pounding reverberated through the house. Both Colin and Ellen ran to the front door. Through the frosted-glass window, they could just make out a dim, blue shape.

"It's your boyfriend." Colin was using the annoying sing-song voice he had adopted every time he spoke of Stephen now.

Ellen suppressed her automatic "He's not my boyfriend." Nothing could stop Colin once he got into teasing her. Anyway, she wasn't sure quite what Stephen was, not since the dance. But the urgent banging on the door was making Ellen fear for the glass.

"Ellen? Ellen!" She pulled the door open. Roger Evans's face was flushed despite the cold, and he was out of breath as if he had been running.

"Thank God!" He seemed to be scanning the hallway behind Ellen. "He's here then, is he?"

Ellen's confusion was slowly turning to fear. Why was Roger banging on her front door like a madman on a Wednesday afternoon? He seemed close to panic, yet almost angry. "Who?" she said. Out of the corner of her eye she could see Colin bouncing up and down as if he was about to say something. "Colin," she said sharply, "haven't you got chores to finish?" Ellen stifled his protest, by adding, "Dad said you don't go out to play until they are done."

Colin trudged theatrically into the kitchen, head hanging, his arms swinging. Ellen slipped out onto the front step, shutting the door firmly behind her.

Roger was shifting from one foot to the other, as if eager to get moving. "Stephen. He's here, isn't he?" Ellen's face must have showed her confusion, because Roger groaned. "Oh, God, tell me he's here!"

"I haven't seen him since the day before yesterday." Ellen shivered. "When the flying was canceled because of the snow, he hitched a ride down here." She smiled. How nervous Stephen had been. He had stood twisting his cap in his hands on the doorstep as if unsure of his welcome. But her smile faded as Roger's words started to penetrate.

"Where could he be? Think, Ellen!" Roger put his hands on Ellen's shoulders and shook her gently, as if this would somehow miraculously produce the answers he wanted.

Freeing herself, Ellen tried to voice the fear that was rising in her. "Why don't you know where he is, Roger? What's happened? Is he all right?"

"I don't know, Ellen. There was a crash today, three chaps killed. Stephen saw it, took it badly. He didn't turn up for ground school. I covered for him, but — they just won't buy it a second time." Roger took his cap off and ran his fingers through his hair. "Look, I've got to get back. If he turns up, send him back sharpish. If he's not back tonight, they'll post him AWOL and he'll wash out." Roger turned and just before he ran off, he said, "It's such a sodding mess, Ellen." His face was wet with tears.

Stephen was safe! Ellen was stunned to find that this had been her fear, ever since she had realized that it was Roger and not Stephen at the door. Her initial euphoria was replaced with anxiety. Where would he have gone? What was he thinking about? Washing out of the course was the greatest fear of any of the trainees. A crash, Ellen thought. Who had been killed? Shuddering, Ellen cursed herself for not even asking Roger. Where could Stephen be?

The front door hit Ellen's back as Colin tried to push it open.

"Get out of the way!" Colin's face was screwed up in mock rage. "You're such a lump, Ellen."

Distractedly, Ellen moved aside to let her brother pass, and then grabbed his collar, yanking him back.

"Oooow. You're strangling me." Colin writhed, but Ellen didn't let up.

"Your chores, are they done?" It was easier to focus on the simple, the everyday.

"Yeah."

"Where are you going? Don't even think about going to your camp, do you understand?"

Colin's camp! Ellen's fingers felt boneless as they fell from Colin's collar. That's where Stephen would be! As Colin muttered something about going over to Jeff's house, Ellen was turning back into the house, talking as she went. "I've got to go out, Colin. I don't know when I'll be back. If I'm not back by the time Mum gets home, tell her I'm at Deanna's to work on our English homework."

"Okay," he said. His lip started to tremble. "Something's happened to Stephen, hasn't it, Ellen?"

Ellen brushed away the tears that were silently trickling down Colin's cheek, and thought of Robbie. "No, he's all right, but I need to find him and talk to him. It's important."

Swallowing his tears, Colin threw his arms around his sister. "I'll stay here till you get back." Sniffling slightly, he added, "If Mum asks questions I'll say that maybe you're staying at Deanna's for dinner." He stepped back abruptly as if surprised to find himself hugging Ellen. "Do you think she'll believe that?"

Trying not to laugh, Ellen said, "I think she will, Colin. After all, it won't be the first time you've lied to her. Come inside, if you're staying. I'll get my coat and boots and get going."

When Ellen finally left, Colin was sitting, uncharacteristically quiet, at the kitchen table, eyeing the cold meat and cold roast potatoes that Ellen had been setting out for dinner when Roger had arrived.

✶   ✶   ✶

As her feet pounded the hard-packed snow, Ellen repeated over and over in her head, "Please, God, let him be there!" Several cars passed, slowing down to see who it was running with such urgency. None of the drivers looked familiar, and she waved them on.

The recent snowfall had shrouded Colin's camp in a fresh covering of white, making it look clean and almost beautiful. On the blanket roof, the snow had mounded and drifted, making the lean-to look like an igloo. Ellen scanned the ground for footprints, but in the growing dusk, it was hard to see. She stepped toward the lean-to. The armchair was empty, like a broken throne. As Ellen got closer, she realized that Stephen was lying in the far corner, curled into a ball in the deeper darkness. His cap had fallen off and his hair was flecked with snow and dirt. His shoulders were shaking and he was sobbing, great gulping sobs that racked his body.

"Stephen?" Ellen whispered, frightened that if she spoke too loudly, he would bolt like a scared animal.

"Go away!" Stephen's voice was thick. He didn't look up.

Ellen moved as quietly as she could until she could hunker down next to him, reaching out tentatively to touch his shoulder. He jerked away so sharply that she lost her balance and went down with a bump. The ground was icy and she felt the cold almost immediately working its way up her legs. She reached out again. This time, Stephen did not jerk away. She let her hand rest on his shoulder. "Stephen? Roger Evans came looking for you. You need to get back to camp."

The sobs were quieter now, but each one still seemed wrenched from Stephen's throat. He said something, but Ellen couldn't make out what it was.

"He told me what happened. I'm sorry. It must have been awful." Even as she spoke, Ellen was conscious of how weak and watery her words sounded.

Stephen reared up, his eyes blazing in his pale face. He spat her words back at her. "Oh, it was awful all right, Ellen!" He shuddered violently and retched, thin strings of bile hanging from his mouth as he leaned over, gasping. Wiping his mouth with the back of one dirty hand, he looked directly at her. "How awful? Did he describe the tearing and grinding as one plane flew into another? Did he tell you about the faces we could see through the canopy, their mouths stretched in screams as the plane fell — the faces of our friends — and there was fuck all we could do?" Stephen grabbed Ellen's shoulders and shook her, hard. "Did he tell you that, Ellen, eh? Did he tell you about the plane hitting the ground? How the ball of flames melted the snow on the field? Did he tell you how we circled aimlessly, watching our friends die because we didn't know what else to bloody do? We'd still be there if the instructor hadn't had to get his damaged plane home. If he hadn't, there'd have been two planes down, not one." Stephen stared at Ellen, but she knew that he didn't see her. "We were practicing formation flying. Three of us — me on the outside, the instructor in the middle, and Lowther on the inside. He just got too close. I could see it happening. I was screaming to Lowther. God knows why, because he couldn't hear. All of us in the plane were shouting. But as I was shouting, I was veering away, because I knew the instructor would have to turn my way. He made it, just, but his wing was damaged. We just watched Lowther go down ... to nothing but flames."

Stephen's grip on Ellen's shoulders relaxed. He smiled at her, and then toppled forward. Ellen held him tightly, grateful for the solid reality of him. His tears soaked her shoulder and hers his hair.

Their trance was broken only when Stephen said, almost conversationally, "I don't think I'm going back, Ellen."

Ellen rocked back on her heels. "What do you mean?"

A strange, almost beatific look appeared on Stephen's face. When he spoke, his voice was measured and calm, although thickened by tears. "They can do what they like to me, but I'm not going to fly anymore. Because if I do, I'm going to die in flames ... just like Lowther."

Scrambling to her feet, Ellen turned and sat in the armchair, facing Stephen. Anger flashed through her. "You're a coward, Stephen Dearborn, a selfish coward!"

Stephen flinched as if Ellen's words were stones flung at him. He remained kneeling, his arms hanging limply at his sides, just staring.

The words were roiling inside Ellen, fighting to get out. "Do you think you're the only one to see men die in this war?" She was speaking so fast that her words ran together. "What about Stewart? Do you think he didn't see dreadful things on that beach at Dieppe? Did he sit down and say he wasn't going to do it anymore, and would they mind putting him on a nice safe ship back home? No, he damn well didn't! He got on with his job." She paused for breath, conscious of how fast her heart was beating. "And what about Lowther? If it had been you who had died, do you think he would be sitting in the woods sobbing and saying he couldn't go on. No! He'd be eager to get on with things, so he could do his part *and* yours." She was running out of steam. Lowther's face, with its happy-go-lucky grin, suddenly appeared over Stephen's. A sob forced its way out. Ellen leaned over and rested her head on her knees, crying.

Stephen's voice seemed to be coming from a long way away, and was curiously uninflected. "I'm so scared, Ellen. You don't know how frightened I sometimes am. I have nightmares about crashing. I've never told anyone about them. I wake up drenched in sweat, shaking. My plane's falling out of the sky and nothing I can do will work."

Lifting her head, Ellen watched Stephen, still on his knees, shuffle over to her.

"Don't think too badly of me," he said, taking her hands in between his. "I can't bear that, Ellen. Not you." His eyes were fixed on her face, pleading.

Ellen suddenly felt very tired. Her anger had gone, and she wasn't sure what she felt now. Thoughts of her brothers, and thoughts of Lowther were all mixed up in her head. It took her a long time to find the words. "Everyone's scared, Stephen," Ellen said. For the first time, Stephen looked young to her, like one of the boys in her class. "All you need to do is just keep going."

Seeing doubt in Stephen's eyes, she went on, "You're a good pilot, aren't you? That's what's needed — good pilots. It's what you joined up for, after all. Besides, think of how much money has been spent on your training. Are you going to waste all that?"

Stephen sighed. "It all sounds so logical, Ellen, when you say it. I just didn't think it would be bloody like this, that's all ..." His voice trailed off. "I never thought about anything but flying, how glorious it would be." Ellen had to strain to hear him. "Planes crash, Ellen, or they get shot down. Men die. There's no glory in that poem, Ellen, the one we liked about the soldier dying and his spirit living on. It's a load of bollocks. When you're dead, you're dead. For Lowther it ended in twisted metal and blood on the snow. That's all there is."

Squeezing Stephen's hands tightly, Ellen willed him to understand the power of what she felt. "Oh, but there is, Stephen! They don't die for nothing. Lowther didn't die for nothing. He died doing something he believed in, so that we can defeat the Nazis, so that we can be free. Just remember, Stephen, what Mr. Churchill said after the Battle of Britain. 'Never has so much been owed to so few.' You're going to be one of those 'few.' You told me you joined up because you wanted desperately to do your bit. I know you can do it, Stephen. I believe in you." The last words were delivered with all the force that Ellen could muster.

Stephen freed his hands and stood up. He walked around, his shoulders drooping, kicking at lumps of snow.

When he finally turned back to her, his face was impassive, but his eyes were still wet. "You're right," was all he said.

"C'mon then!" Ellen forced enthusiasm into her voice and jumped up quickly, not wanting Stephen to have time to change his mind. "Let's get you back to camp, before poor Roger has to cover for you again. He was in a dreadful state." Ellen punched Stephen lightly on the shoulder. "He was there, too, remember. And I'd say he got the heebie-jeebies as well, only he showed it differently. That's what you have, the heebie-jeebies." Ellen pulled Stephen along behind her. "Once you're up in your plane again, you'll be back to normal, you'll see."

"Yes. The heebie-jeebies, the jitters, call them what you will!" Stephen's voice was loud in the quiet of the early evening. "I'll be fine, Ellen. Don't you worry about me." He forced a laugh. "Got to be the dashing pilot, to impress the girls, what!" he said, twirling an imaginary handlebar mustache.

They had come to the fork in the road that led to the camp. Stephen turned, kissed her cheek, a little peck of a kiss. Ellen took his head in her hands and kissed him firmly on the lips. His mouth tasted salty. Stephen ran toward the camp. Without looking back, he raised one hand in a wave.

Ellen watched his small, stocky figure until it disappeared into the darkness.

TWELVE

1445326 LAC S. Dearborn
SFTS 16
Hagersville
Ontario
Canada

9th of January, 1943

Dear Mum, Dad and Dorrie,

The last few days have been hard for us all here. While practising formation flying, my friend Lowther and two other trainees were killed. You can imagine, I'm sure, how we all are feeling. You, in particular, Dad. If it hadn't been for my friend Ellen I would have found it hard to get through. She's been a brick. We talk about the future, how we are both going to teach after the war. That helps.

Lowther was a good friend to me — perhaps

more than I realised. He was older than the rest of us and has a wife back in New Zealand, and a little son. Everyone says that they're going to write to her, tell her what a jolly good bloke he was, but most won't. I will, though. It's snowing again so all flying has been canceled, just for a change.

I miss you all, more than I can say. There's still talk that our course might not have done enough flying to pass out because of all this snow. I'm just hoping that's not the case, because I'm longing to be back in England and to hug you all.

Your loving son,
Stephen

P.S. Don't worry about me. I'm all right, really, just a bit down in the dumps.

☆   ☆   ☆

1445326 LAC S. Dearborn
SFTS 16
Hagersville
Ontario
Canada

9th of January, 1943

Dear Mrs. Lowther,
This is the sixth go I've had at writing this

letter. I tried starting off with all the usual things people say about how sorry they are for your loss, but I couldn't get any further, because it all sounded so stilted and formal. George would have hated that — he would have laughed at me and called me a pompous little twerp. So, here goes, I'm just going to write what I feel and not worry about whether it's proper form.

It feels funny calling him George, but I'm sure that's what you would have called him. We called him just plain Lowther, or Kiwi, or sometimes Daddy Lowther. That was a joke because he was the oldest on the course, but it wasn't really a joke. I can tell you this because I'm smuggling this letter to a friend off the base, and she's going to post it for me. That way it won't go through the censor, because what I'm going to tell you could get me kicked out. You see, I lied about my age when I joined up. When I first met your husband, I was sixteen. (I had my seventeenth birthday just before Christmas.) He never said anything, but I think he suspected. It didn't stop him ragging me at times — he had a wicked sense of humour, as I'm sure you well know — but he was also very kind and he looked out for me. Sometimes I have nightmares and the others give me a hard time, because I make such a racket. After the first couple of times, he'd tell them to knock it off and leave me alone. I'm going to miss him.

We all are. He was the one who got things

going, always joking, or up for an outing to town.
But I know that none of us will miss him as much
as you and your son. He didn't talk much about
you; none of us talk about our families really. But,
the day after our New Year's Eve dance, he and I
were the only ones in the barracks. He showed
me the pictures you'd just sent him. The one
where you're standing by a sea wall holding up
your son — that was the one he really liked. He
said he was going to keep it in his wallet, so that
he would remember what he was fighting for and
what he would be coming home to. He laughed
at Jock's little fists, like a little prizefighter, thought
he was definitely a chip off the old block.

I had taken my first girl to that dance. Ellen
Logan's her name. She started out just a friend,
but I think I feel something more for her now.
George liked her, even though he teased me about
her. He said that she was a lot like you, "his Pat,"
he called you. I wasn't sure what he meant at first,
because she's sandy haired and you're dark, but
he said that it was in character. Ellen's quiet, even
a bit moody at times, but George said that
underneath she was a strong character, even if she
didn't know it yet.

I was there when George's plane went down.
It was a fluke accident. It couldn't have been
prevented, just one of those things that happens
sometimes. He didn't suffer at all. Our instructor
says they were all killed instantly. I had a hard time

thinking about George's death at first. It seemed so pointless. Maybe you're thinking like that, too. I don't know. But it wasn't, not really. My friend Ellen has convinced me it wasn't. George volunteered because he believed it was the right thing to do. He died training to make the world a better place for you and Jock. We have to believe that.

I don't know what else to say. Lowther was a good friend and a fine man. I know you'll tell Jock that as he grows up. It's important that he knows.

Yours sincerely,
Stephen Dearborn (Swee'Pea)

* * *

Ellen,

I'm sending this note with Evans. I can't come over this evening after all. I'm struggling with the stuff I missed that day (you know which one I mean), so I'd better hit the books. I'm really sorry. If it continues snowing I don't think we'll be flying again tomorrow. Maybe your mum could feed a hungry airman that day instead? Evans is also bringing you my copy of *The Wind in the Willows*. In it, you'll find the aerogram I've written to Lowther's wife. Could you post it for me? I'd ask Evans to, but he might ask questions about why I didn't want the censor to see it. I'm sure you can guess why. I think writing it was the hardest thing I've ever done. I wished I could have talked to you as I wrote. You have the knack of making things seem so simple.

Stephen

✷   ✷   ✷

The huge wind was terrifying. It howled past the fuselage of the plane, battering Stephen's ears and taking his breath away. A greenish-gray fog seemed to envelop everything.

Stephen could just make out the other plane flying alongside on his right. Strangely, it wasn't yellow like all the training planes. It wasn't even the familiar Avro Anson. Dredging through his mind, Stephen finally came up with the name — Halifax. The great, lumbering plane beside him was a Halifax bomber! Peering out through the perspex of his canopy, Stephen could see a vast flight of the planes, dotted blackly against the sky.

A flicker of movement in the cockpit of the plane alongside him caught his eye. The pilot was looking in his direction and waving frantically. It was Lowther. He was giving Stephen the thumbs-up sign. Even at this distance, Stephen could see that Lowther was smiling broadly. Then he pointed down, indicating that Stephen should look at an area on the fuselage just below the cockpit. There, in colors, vibrant even in the odd murky air, was a painting of a pin-up girl. She had dark, curly hair. Underneath was written in elaborate script, "Peerless Pat." Stephen laughed and looked up, gesturing with one hand to show Lowther that he had seen it.

His mouth opened in horror, but no sound came out. In the few seconds he had looked away, the planes had come perilously close together. He waved to Lowther, trying to tell him to back off, but Lowther continued to smile. Stephen tried to bank to the left, but the controls were all dead in his hands. Nothing happened. He could feel beads of sweat breaking out on his forehead. He let his trembling hands remain on the useless controls, praying that they would suddenly spring to life again. The Halifax moved inexorably closer. Lowther's beaming smile grew even broader. Stephen braced himself for the impact he knew was coming. It was surprisingly loud. The small Anson shuddered and bucked as the larger plane ground into it, shearing off its right wing. In the few seconds before his plane began to spin out of control, Stephen felt strangely calm as he watched the Halifax gradually fade into the mist.

All the switches and dials in front of him meant nothing. Stephen looked down at his hands, clumsy in leather gauntlets, clutching the stick. Tentatively, he lifted one, watched how slowly it moved. The air had solidified and it took all his strength to push through it. He pulled hard back. Nothing happened.

The wind was getting louder. There was a metallic screaming that hurt Stephen's ears. At first he thought the plane was breaking apart, then he realized that he was making the noise, a high-pitched, keening wail that tore his throat. Through the windscreen of the cockpit, he could no longer see sky, just the brown and green blur of the ground that was hurtling toward him. Instinctively, Stephen threw his *hands in front of his face, knowing, even as he did it, that it was useless. Nothing could save him now.*

With a shudder, Stephen jolted awake and lay unmoving, staring up at the bottom of Lowther's bunk. It was undisturbed. He would have to get used to that — no more shifting positions from Lowther now. His heart was racing and, despite the frigid air in the barrack room, he was sweating, so much that his flannel pajamas were sodden. He held his hand in front of his face, half surprised to see that it was ungloved. The nightmare. He hadn't had it for a while, but now it was back in all its sweaty, gut-churning glory.

Stephen shuddered and turned over so that he faced the wall. He closed his eyes, knowing that he wouldn't sleep. Something was missing. It took him a few seconds to realize that he was listening for Lowther's bubbling snore.

THIRTEEN

"No." Deanna shook her head. "I'm not going to come, and that's it." She sucked hard on the straw in her chocolate milk shake. Her brown hair fell forward, hiding her face from Ellen and Barb, who sat on either side of her at the soda fountain in Courtnage's.

Ellen and Barb exchanged a look over their friend's bent head. "I don't understand," Ellen said. "You love parties, Deanna, and that's all this is, a farewell party for Stephen, Roger and some of the other English boys."

Deanna looked sideways at Ellen, a mulish look on her face. "What's the point of going to a farewell party for people I don't know?" she said triumphantly. "What do you want to do, introduce me to them just in time to say good-bye?"

"No, that does sound stupid." Ellen placed a placatory hand on Deanna's arm. "We want you there because you're our friend, and we'll all have a good time. Dad's said we can take the furniture out of the parlor, roll back the carpet and set up the gramophone so we can dance."

Barb had just started to add her plea to Ellen's when Deanna sat up straight, pushed away her glass and turned on Ellen. Two spots of color looked as if they had been painted on her pale cheeks. Her eyes were glistening. "I'm your friend, am I? Funny that for the last two months you two haven't had time for your 'friend' except at school. You're always with Stephen and Roger, whenever they can get away from the camp." Pausing, she looked directly at Barb. "And you're the worst, hanging round the camp gate when he can't get away. Oh, I know all about that, Barb!"

Involuntarily, Ellen drew in her breath in shock.

Deanna rounded on her. "Didn't you know what she's been getting up to? She's as bad as Patsy Grant. In fact, it was Patsy who told me."

Bristling, Barb returned Deanna's accusing stare. "So what? He's not here for long. We've always known that and we want to make use of what little time we've got. You're just jealous, Deanna, and, anyway, it's not like we didn't ask you to come with us when we went to the Regah Cinema or here for a soda. You always said no."

Deanna had half risen from her seat, but flopped back down, resting her head on her hands. "Well, it hasn't been much fun, being a fifth wheel, when both of you have boyfriends, and I haven't." She raised a hand. "I know, you say he's just a friend, Ellen. But I've seen the two of you together, and whether you admit it or not, Stephen's more than a friend!"

Ellen couldn't think of anything to say. It was true. In the past two months, she had spent a lot of time with Stephen. He spent most of his off-duty time at her house, much of it spent talking or reading together. But he seemed content with that. Ever since Lowther's death, he had been withdrawn at times, and he had never once touched her, not since she had been so bold and kissed him on that dreadful day. Sometimes Ellen almost wished he would, but then she thought back to Barb's stories of Roger of the Roving Hands, and knew that she didn't want that. She sighed. Everything about Stephen was so confusing.

"Look, Deanna, if you feel we've neglected you lately, then I'm sorry. It wasn't intentional. You're my friend and I'd like you to come. Your parents will be there, so you'd be all by yourself at home." Ellen looked earnestly at her friend.

A small smile twitched Deanna's lips. "Oh, all right," she said, "I'll come." She laughed. "But there's one condition. Stephen and Roger have to bring along someone from one of the courses behind them, someone who's not being shipped out of here any time soon. Someone tall, like Roger, not a shortie like Stephen, okay?"

Ellen grinned, a broad grin that was tinged with relief. "We'll see what we can do, won't we, Barb?"

Distractedly, Barb nodded. She picked up her schoolbag and stood up. "Look, I've got to go. I'll see you tomorrow night." She hurried out, her head down.

Looking at each other in puzzlement, Ellen and Deanna gathered their belongings. "What's up with her?" Deanna asked, as if Ellen should know the reason for Barb's abruptness.

"Beats me," Ellen said. "Barb's been moody for the last week. Sometimes she's fine — the quiet, funny Barb we know. Other times, she's miles away, not listening to a word you say, or she's really grumpy." She made a face. "It's probably just that Roger and Stephen are being sent home, now that they've completed their training."

She linked her arm through Deanna's and pulled her out the door into the street. "They're having their graduation parade today, when they get their wings. I wish I could see it. Stephen's going to be a sergeant. If he'd got better marks, he'd be a pilot officer like Roger."

"Does he mind?" Deanna asked.

"A bit." Ellen shrugged. "They'll end up doing the same thing, flying bombers or fighters, depending where they're posted. Stephen's convinced he's going to be on bombers. All he hopes is that he'll be in England, so he can see his family. He'll know today." Her face darkened. "I just hope he stays safe."

Ellen shook herself. "Why don't you come home with me, Dee? Help me make food for the party tomorrow. I want to do some tonight, because Stephen's asked me to go to Hamilton tomorrow. We're going to shop for some presents for his family, have some lunch and then come back in time for the party."

There was a lightness in Ellen's voice as she continued. "He and Roger are staying over tomorrow night, sleeping in the boys' old room."

Deanna stopped walking. "I'll come, but you know, Ellen, Barb was right. I am a bit jealous." Her face was thoughtful. "No, wait. I was jealous, but I don't think I am anymore. I'd hate to have to say good-bye like this, not knowing what was going to happen."

✻   ✻   ✻

Ellen shivered slightly, pulling her coat collar tight around her chin. A crowd was milling around outside Courtnage's, waiting for the bus to Hamilton. She could see some of her mother's friends, but most were trainees from the base. Although she didn't know their names, Ellen recognized faces from the dance and suspected that many of them were from Stephen's course, off to celebrate their graduation. New stripes had been hastily sewn on to sleeves, and some proudly wore peaked officers' caps instead of the usual forage cap. She stamped her feet, looking anxiously around. Where was Stephen? It was unlike him to be late. She'd be mad if he stood her up. Ellen had never been to Hamilton without either her parents or one of her older brothers. She still found it hard to believe that her parents were allowing her to go, but she supposed that they thought of Stephen as another Stewart or Graham. Ellen's mother had been full of suggestions about where to shop — Eaton's being her top choice.

Ellen felt a tap on her left shoulder. She spun round, but no one was there. Looking round, she saw Roger Evans standing on her right, laughing. Stephen stood a few paces behind him, looking solemn.

"Tricked you!" Roger's grin was infectious. "Bet you thought he wasn't coming." He pushed Stephen forward. "Aren't you going to give her a kiss?"

Stephen's face flushed a dull, brick red.

Roger seemed oblivious to his friend's discomfort. "He's a sergeant now. First chance you'll get to kiss a sergeant, Ellen!" He looked at the pair of them. "I don't know what to make of you two, I really don't. He's miserable if he doesn't see you, but then I have to drag him here this morning, because he's in some kind of funk he doesn't want to talk about." Roger's grin took on an edge of malice. "You know what? I could order him to kiss you now. What do you think of that?"

Ellen and Stephen were saved from having to think about it by the timely arrival of the bus. She had already got their tickets, so it was just a matter of getting on and finding a seat. Without so much as a look at Roger, Stephen grabbed Ellen's hand and roughly pulled her into the crush of people at the door. Ellen turned and waved to Roger, who tipped his cap jauntily before setting off down the road toward Barb's house.

By judicious use of his elbows, Stephen secured them two seats. He let Ellen take the one by the window before flopping down heavily next to her. "Evans can be such a prat!"

Surprised by the vehemence of his words, Ellen asked, "Why do you say that? I thought you liked him."

"Oh, he's all right most of the time, but everything's a big joke as far as he's concerned." Stephen was slumped in his seat, causing the collar of his greatcoat to ride up. He looked like a turtle trying to hide in its shell. "He just got my goat on the way over, making wisecracks about all the girls who would be after him now that he's an officer, how he'd be fighting them off once we got back to England."

Ellen flinched, thinking of how Barb's eyes softened whenever she talked about Roger Evans. Maybe that was why she had been so moody. "What did he mean when he said you were in a funk? I thought you'd be really happy today, Stephen. After all, isn't this what you've been working for?"

"Oh, it's nothing." Stephen avoided Ellen's smile and looked out of the window. "You know what a moody bugger I can be." He sat up straighter, took a deep breath and added, "I was just a bit sad that there was no one watching for me at the passing-out parade yesterday. I'd have liked my Old Man to be there, that's all." The words came out quickly.

Ignoring her concerned scrutiny, Stephen's voice was determinedly hearty. "So, Miss Logan! Where are you going to take me to spend my carefully hoarded pennies?"

Ellen knew her concern was being dismissed, but she also knew that if Stephen didn't want to talk about something, nothing would make him. "Eaton's for your mum and Dorrie. We can get them some silk stockings — I know those are hard to get in England. We can probably get something for your nephew there, too, in the toy department. Your dad's going to be hard, though."

"We'll find something, even if we have to visit every shop." There was relief in Stephen's voice, as though he was glad to be talking about small, inconsequential things.

✫   ✫   ✫

Ellen eventually lost count of the shops they visited, but it was headily exciting to be out alone with Stephen.

She was conscious of the looks people gave them and was glad that she had worn her best coat, even if it was a little warm for the weather. Stephen's uniform with its achingly new sergeant's stripes eased them into conversations wherever they went. Everyone wanted to know how long he had been in Canada, and where he was going to be posted. As he shyly answered their questions, Ellen wondered whether Stephen's moodiness was because she had not asked him about his posting herself. She knew he was longing to be based close to London, so he would have a chance to see his family. RAF Lissett was what he told people, but Ellen had no clue as to where that might be. Stephen's departure was not something she felt comfortable thinking about, let alone talking about. I'm as bad as Stephen, Ellen thought.

The center of Hamilton was crowded with Saturday shoppers, and after a while, Ellen felt overwhelmed. She had lost herself for more than a few minutes in a pile of used books on display outside a shop, but now her feet were hurting and the lunch she and Stephen had had at The Chicken Roost seemed a long time ago. They had to get out to Dundas by 3:00 P.M. so that they could ride back to Hagersville with her aunt and her family. Glancing at her watch, Ellen saw that it was already 1:30 P.M. She looked round to tell Stephen they should be heading for the station soon. He was nowhere in sight. Ellen frantically scanned the crowds, hoping to catch sight of the familiar blue uniform. Finally, she spotted him coming out of a store. Pushing her way through the throngs that seemed determined to hinder her progress, Ellen made it to Stephen's side, as he hastily shoved something in his trouser pocket.

"Don't run away like that, Stephen. You scared me."

He looked guilty, his cheeks flushed, but he blustered back. "Me? You were the one who got your nose stuck in those books. I got bored and came to look for something for Dad." He waved awkwardly at the store behind him.

"A jewelry store! What on earth could you find for him in there?" Her worry made the scorn in Ellen's voice stronger than she had intended it to be.

Staring at the ground, Stephen muttered, "Oh, I don't know, maybe a hip flask or something. He could take it with him when he's on duty as an air raid warden."

"Did you find one?"

Stephen shook his head, "Too expensive." He suddenly grinned. "Even though I'm now earning the princely sum of thirteen shillings a day!" Stephen grabbed her hand and started off through the crowds. "Being such a rich toff, I'll treat you to a tea and sticky bun at the station while we wait for the train. What do you say to that?"

☆　　☆　　☆

Dusk was falling by the time the overloaded car drew up outside the Logans' house. It had taken an age for Ellen's aunt to organize her three young children. Her uncle had been busy fussing with the car, so she and Stephen had sat on the porch making desultory conversation. Stephen had sat with his back against one of the wooden support pillars, staring up at the escarpment that loomed over her aunt's house. Ellen had sat beside him, her coat wrapped around her drawn-up knees.

"Lissett. Where's Lissett? That's where you said you were being posted, isn't it?"

"Yorkshire, I think." Stephen's voice had been quiet, his whole demeanor subdued.

"Can you get home from there easily?" Ellen had followed Stephen's gaze and watched a hawk spiral on air currents, high above their heads.

"It's not a short journey, so it won't be worth it for

a 48-hour pass; but for a longer leave, there's bound to be someone with a car who'll be heading for the fleshpots of London. I'll be able to scrounge a lift."

"Stephen, look —" Ellen had half turned toward him. "You must think I'm awful for not even asking you this stuff this morning. I meant to …" Her voice had trailed off. She had tried again. "It's just that if I don't think about you going, then I can pretend it's not happening." She'd wondered whether Stephen had heard her, so intently had he been staring at the hawk. "What will you be flying?" Practical details were safe.

"Halifaxes or Lancasters. I'll be with Bomber Command."

Bomber Command. She had looked out at the peaceful streets of Dundas, imagined bombs raining down on them, and shivered.

"Let's not think about all that now." Stephen had still stared straight ahead, but Ellen had sensed that he was as conscious of her as she was of him. "Tell me what you are going to do again when the war is over."

"Oh, Stephen!" Ellen had shrugged. "You know what I want — we've talked about this so many times — to go to university and study English, but Dad won't budge about me staying in school now. The only way I can see it happening is if I go to night school or save every penny until I can afford to quit my job and just do it."

"It'll be easier for me," Stephen had said. "I'd like to go to London University — that's where my teacher, Mr. Topham, went — to study French and then teach."

"Easier then, but not easier now," Ellen's voice had quavered. "What you've got to face is far worse than anything that'll happen to me. Why, I can't imagine —"

Stephen had stood up abruptly, and walked over to where a ball lay abandoned on the grass. He had picked it up, tossed it from hand to hand. "Never mind that, Ellen. There's something else I want to ask you."

"That's my ball! Put it down!" George, Ellen's six-year-old cousin, had barreled down the path and launched himself at Stephen, who had dropped the ball and swung the angry child into the air. There his shouts had turned quickly to laughter as Stephen tickled him and tussled with him.

Seeing a crowd of people peering out her front door, Ellen wondered whether there would be a quiet time this evening when she could find out what it was that Stephen had wanted to ask her.

✳   ✳   ✳

Ellen never thought of her parents' house as small, but tonight it seemed crowded. Everywhere she turned, people were jammed together. The older men had gathered on the verandah, close to the keg of beer that had been set up there. Clouds of cigarette and pipe smoke surrounded them. The women were in the dining-room, talking in groups or fussing around the buffet laid out on the pristine dining-room table, where the jewel colors of Jell-O shone. Colin and a motley crew of cousins and younger brothers and sisters were tearing excitedly around the backyard, happy to be up past their bedtime. About five of Stephen and Roger's fellow trainees had turned up — as Roger put it, "the quiet ones who weren't keen on a drunken bash in Hamilton." They were surrounded by Ellen's school friends — the girls gazing at them with frank admiration and the boys quizzing them about their training. Ellen grinned to see Deanna positioned close to the tallest of them, a lanky Rhodesian who seemed not unhappy to have such a persistent admirer.

Roger was fiddling with Stewart's gramophone, Barb patiently by his side. As the gramophone blared into life, Deanna grabbed the Rhodesian's hand and pulled him into the small space that had been cleared for dancing. Others quickly followed, and soon it was jam-packed. Ellen suggested that maybe she and Stephen sit this one out, but he appeared not to hear her. With his arm around her waist, he quickly had them in the thick of the melee. Roger had turned the gramophone up so loud that it was hard to talk, and Stephen seemed miles away, content to hold Ellen in his arms and shuffle around. Ellen suspected it was Roger who turned off the parlor lights, leaving the dancers in the dim light that shone from the hallway.

They must have been dancing for almost three quarters of an hour when the music came to an abrupt stop and the lights came on. Ellen's father stood in the doorway, a full pint mug in his hand. Behind him were clustered all the other grown-ups. The children had lined up around the walls, clutching sticky glasses of ginger ale.

"Everyone, I'd like you all to charge your glasses, and then I'd like to say a few words." Bill Logan's Scottish burr was more pronounced than usual. Ellen watched him as everyone scrambled to get drinks, noting from the flush on his face that he had had more than usual to drink. Stephen reappeared at her side, a glass of beer in one hand, a lemonade for Ellen in the other. She gratefully sipped the cool, tart drink.

As everyone settled down and turned expectantly toward the doorway, Mr. Logan lifted his glass up above his head. "I'd like to propose a toast." He grinned and shook his head at a shouted comment from one his cronies from the Legion. "I'll keep it short, that I promise. I'd like you all to raise your glasses and drink a toast to all our young friends here who have now got their wings and are going to go and give Jerry hell!" He laughed and winked at his wife. "Heck, I mean." The smile vanished, and Ellen suddenly noticed how tired and drawn her father looked. "Joking aside, we owe a lot to these young men. They're sacrificing their youths and leaving their families behind to take on a difficult fight." With a meaningful look at Ellen, he added, "We can all learn from their example."

Ellen felt rather than saw Stephen tense. His mouth was open as if he was going to say something, but she took hold of his arm and shook her head.

Ellen's father, unaware of Stephen's disquiet, continued, raising his glass higher. "Let's drink to our boys in blue! And in particular, to Stephen Dearborn, who's become like a son to us." With that, he took a large gulp of his beer. The toast was echoed around the room, then a buzz of conversation rose so that Ellen was unable to hear what Stephen said as he turned and abruptly left the house.

*   *   *

After the bright lights of the house, it was difficult for Ellen's eyes to adjust to the darkness outside. The garden was strangely quiet and there was no sign of Stephen. Avoiding the children trickling out to resume their games, Ellen walked around the house. Farther down the road, sitting on the curb, she spotted a small, stocky figure.

Ellen ran to join Stephen, sitting down next to him, not caring whether her dress got dirty.

He sat with his knees apart, his hands loosely clasped. He looked sideways at Ellen and grinned ruefully.

"He means well, you know," Ellen said, "and he *is* very fond of you."

"I know," Stephen said simply. "I like your dad, but why does he have that blind spot about you, Ellen? Why has he got this bee in his bonnet about you leaving school?"

Ellen understood her father, but that didn't mean that it hurt any less. "It's not just me, Stephen. He's old fashioned about a woman's place. It's only the war that's let him accept the idea of Mum doing stuff other than being a housewife. I'd have had a fight on my hands even if he hadn't found out about girls leaving school early to do war work. He's stubborn." She laughed. "So am I. I take after him in that. I'll get there in the end — it just will take longer, that's all."

Stephen fumbled in his pocket and brought out a small box. He thrust it awkwardly at Ellen, causing the box to bump against her closed fist. When he spoke, Ellen could hear a catch in his voice. "I was going to give you this tomorrow when we walked back to the camp, but maybe now's the time. Maybe it might change your dad's mind."

Confusion caused Ellen's fingers to be clumsy as she opened the box. Inside, nestled in a slit cut in the white silk lining, lay a small ring. At its center was a crown of gold surmounting a crest on which the letters RAF had been embossed; on either side, a plumed wing ran down into the shank. Ellen traced the patterns with her finger.

"Ellen."

Stephen got no further. Ellen, tears welling in her eyes, shook her head. A feeling was building inside her that if Stephen continued, everything would change forever.

"Don't," she finally blurted out, through a small sob. "Don't say any more, please!"

"Oh, hell! This isn't going right." Stephen kicked his foot against the curb. His voice was clotted with tears.

"I knew I'd blow it. I just don't know how to handle this, Ellen. I can't just leave you like this. I want —." He broke off, shaking his head. "Damn, I don't really know what I want, but ..."

Ellen felt as if a wind was blowing through her, stirring up feelings that she had tried to ignore so that everything would stay the same. "No!" she whispered, hating the way Stephen's face crumpled in on itself, and forcing herself to try and explain the emotions whirling inside her. "You're leaving me here. There's nothing we can do to change that. But I'll write. I promise I'll write, every day, if that's what you want." Ellen heard the note of pleading in her voice, and willed Stephen to hear it, too, to understand the depth of her feelings for him that she was scared to articulate. She leaned over and took his hand. "That's the best for both of us, Stephen. We're just so young — and we don't know what's going to happen." Forcing him to turn and face her, Ellen continued, looking directly into Stephen's eyes. "Will that be enough?"

Stephen leaned forward so his forehead rested on Ellen's. "I don't know, Ellen. I really don't know. What I do know is that you're the only person I can talk to about how I really feel. With the other chaps, it's all stiff upper lip — anything else is just not done. With Mum, Dad and Dorrie, I can't let them know if I'm scared or worried, because then they'll worry, too." Ellen felt a shudder run through him. "You've seen me at my worst, Ellen, when I was blubbing like a baby." Stephen snorted, and Ellen felt his warm breath on her face.

"And you still like me, even when I'm moody and down in the dumps. I couldn't bear to lose that."

Ellen straightened up, looking at Stephen's downcast head. The pinkness of his neck with the sharply razored line of hair above it reminded her of Colin. She held out the ring box to him. "You don't have to, Stephen."

"No, keep it, Ellen. I want you to keep it. Wear it on a chain round your neck if you like." He stood up and linked their arms, a small smile working hard to stay on his serious face. "Maybe one day you'll decide you can wear it on your finger." Stephen started back toward the Logans' house, which was ablaze with lights. "Just promise me you'll write."

Ellen thrust the ring box into the pocket of her dress, feeling it bump against her thigh with each step. "I never break a promise, Stephen," she said quietly.

FOURTEEN

200 King Street
Hagersville
Ontario
Canada

18th of March, 1943

Dear Stephen,

I'm keeping my promise. Though if I am
honest, it's a struggle. Don't get all huffy — it's not
that I don't want to write to you. I do! But I don't
think I can write to you every day. Nothing
happens here. I have absolutely nothing to tell you
other than Colin's latest mischief, and that's going
to wear pretty thin. Much more exciting things
must be happening to you. Fancy sailing back to
England on the *Queen Elizabeth*. Was it as luxurious
as it looked in all those newsreels from before the
war? Did you get seasick? I'm sure I would.

My Uncle Rob took us out on Lake Ontario last
year and I was so sick that my mother said I'd
turned green. Can you imagine — with my hair
and freckles? Now you definitely won't want me
writing to you!

Everyone here sends their love. Mum has
been much happier because we've been getting
letters more regularly from Stewart. He seems
okay, although sometimes he sounds very down.
He hasn't said much about how badly he was
wounded, only that he took shrapnel in the
arm and chest. We send him parcels through the
Red Cross, but who knows if they get through.
Graham's squadron has been posted to County
Durham. Is that near where you are going to be?

You haven't been gone that long, but I already
miss you. I've been reading the books you left.
I come across things that make me laugh and I
know that you would have laughed, too. I really
like the H.G. Wells stories, especially "Kipps."
I imagine your voice whenever Kipps is talking.
That must mean Wells is a good author, to get
a character's voice so real like that. Do all
Londoners sound like you?

You must be so excited about seeing your
mum, dad and Dorrie. How long will you be able
to stay with them before you have to join your
squadron? What a stroke of luck that Dorrie's
husband, Ron, has got some leave, too. It will be
the first time you've all been together for more

than a year. Don't forget your Canadian family —
we will be thinking of you, too.

Best wishes,
Ellen

P.S. Did Roger travel over to England with you?
Barb hasn't heard from him and she wondered if
you had an address for him.

P.P.S. I nearly forgot. The Girls Athletic Association
at school is sponsoring a tea dance. If you'd been
here, I'd have asked you.

✯   ✯   ✯

1445326 Sgt. S. Dearborn
C/o 79 Gellately Road
New Cross
London
England

29th of March, 1943

Dear Ellen,
    Your letters have kept me going, but I understand
that writing every day was a bit optimistic and that it
was becoming a bit of a bind. And, no, I didn't get
huffy when you told me that you were going to
write less often — just pouted a bit!

You wouldn't believe what a wonderful time I've had here at home. Talk about the conquering hero and, blimey, I haven't even done anything yet. All my relatives came the first weekend, and we had a right old knees-up. The Old Man was positively jolly. He's peculiar. He acts now like he never threw such a wobbly about me joining up. He doesn't say much, but I can tell he's proud of me. He took me to work the other day, and to his ARP post to introduce me to all his colleagues. I've even been down to the Duke of Clarence with him a couple of times, even though we're neither of us big drinkers. We sit there in silence for the most part, but every so often he huffs into his moustache and throws out a question. Wanted to know what I had planned for after the war. I didn't hold back, Ellen. I thought I'd better tell him straight that I'm going into teaching. He took it well enough. Said that all he wanted for me was a job where I could use my brains and where I wouldn't get my hands dirty and have to do heavy labour, like he's done all his life. That made me understand why he was so upset when I chucked school in. It's funny when you think about it: here's my dad upset because I left school early, and there's yours doing all he can to push you out early.

The only bad thing is that Mum's arthritis is really playing her up. She and Dorrie only let on the half of it in their letters, but she's hardly able to walk now. Spends most of her time on the sofa in the back parlour. It's hard on Dorrie, too, as she has to do all the housework, and Andrew's a scamp, rather like your Colin. I gave him a bit of a talking to, and told him how he had to mind his mum and help out more now that he's getting to be a big boy. I promised him that if I got good reports about him, I'd send him some pocket money each week. You should have seen his little face light up. I offered to send Mum and Dorrie an allowance each week, too, but they said they don't need it, told me to save it for my education. You wouldn't believe it — I get four pounds, fourteen shillings a week now. I'm rolling in it, and it's not like I've got much to spend it on, so I can save a fair bit.

I was glad to hear that letters from your Stewart are getting through. Don't get upset if he seems down, though. Think what it must be like for him, stuck in the same place all the time, the Germans in charge, and nothing very much to do. It'd be enough to get anyone down. Remember how lonely and blue I was until your family took me in, and I wasn't even in prison!

Barb hasn't heard from Evans. That's too bad, but maybe you can try and let her down gently. I don't think she will hear. Oh, he was keen to start with, that's for sure, pestering the living daylights out of me, but I sensed it was the thrill of the chase that he wanted, and that he was cooling off toward the end of our stay. He's still in Canada, as far as I know. Got sent on some hush–hush course out in British Columbia.

As to you looking a sight when you turned green, that wouldn't matter to me, Ellen. I like your freckles. I've been showing my snaps of you to all my family. Ron says to tell you that you remind him of Deanna Durbin! Now that can't be too bad, can it?

You can send your letters here, if you like, until I get settled. Dorrie will send them on, and once I get my new address sorted out, you can guarantee you'll be one of the first to get it. I'm a bit apprehensive about joining the squadron. I know I can do the flying — or I will be able to once I've put in a few hours on Halifaxes. It's the crew that worries me. How will I get on with them? They're all bound to be older than me — not that they'll know that, of course. Worse is them depending on me. That's a hell of a responsibility.

Ah, damn it, I'm going all gloomy on you, Ellen. I promised myself I wouldn't do that. Not after you saw me through all that stuff in January. I'll be fine.

Your loving friend,
Stephen

☆　　☆　　☆

200 King Street
Hagersville
Ontario
Canada

20th of June, 1943

Dear Stephen,

So many letters! How do you find the time? I know, you said in your last letter, "When you're not on a raid, there's sod all else to do!" I blushed when I read that and even more when I wrote it! Your language has got worse since you joined that squadron. In fact, you sound different altogether. Is it getting to you a bit? I wish you'd tell me more about how you feel. I like the way you describe your crew — you really make them come alive for me — but I worry about how you're coping. It must be such a strain, but you don't say much about that. Still, you'll be due for some leave soon, and will get to see your family. I was thrilled to hear that Dorrie and Ron are going to have a baby at the end of the year. What a wonderful Christmas present!

That brings me to something that's hard to write, but I think you should know as you might run into Roger Evans again. Barb is going to have a baby, too, only not in such happy circumstances. When I told her that you didn't have an address for him, she got really down. She's been moody for a while, but Deanna and I just put it down to her missing Roger and him giving her the cold shoulder. About a month ago, she was away from school for a couple of days. When I went over to her place, her mother said she had stomach flu and she'd be back at the beginning of the week. When she didn't show on Monday morning, I stopped off on my way home. (Deanna didn't come because she was working on the yearbook.) There was no answer, but I saw the curtains twitch, so I knew someone was there. I rang the bell again, and knocked on the door. Finally, Barb answered. She looked awful, Stephen, her eyes all swollen from crying, her nose red. It would have broken your heart to see her. At first, I thought that maybe she'd had some bad news, maybe that Roger was dead. When I asked what was wrong, she just started sobbing. I didn't know what to do.

Eventually, I got her settled in the kitchen while I made her some tea. She just kept crying. When I finally asked her if Roger was all right, she burst out, "I hate him!" She told me everything then. What was it you called him? A prat? He's that for sure. Barb used to call him Roger of the Roving Hands, but because she made a joke of it, I thought … well, you know. It makes me so angry, Stephen. He blackmailed her into letting him make love to her — there's no other way to describe it. He kept on and on about how dangerous flying was, how he had no idea whether he would survive the war, and how he loved her and wanted them to be together. Well, I don't think I have to spell it out. Barb hadn't told anyone about the baby, not even Roger, although I think she might have suspected that she was pregnant around the time you shipped out.

She was so scared. She knew she wouldn't be able to keep it a secret much longer. I told her she had to tell her parents. She said that they'd kill her. I know, people just say that, but she was shaking so hard I offered to be there when she told them. I nearly cried then, too, because Barb gave me one of those watery, quivery smiles you do when you're crying and said that I'd just be letting myself in for a whole load of trouble. So I left after she promised she'd tell them. I might as well have stayed, because I got the trouble anyway, but more of that later. Let me finish telling you what's happened to Barb. Her parents whisked her away the next day. They say she's gone to her aunt's in Toronto, to help her out while her uncle's overseas as her aunt's got a toddler and a baby on the way. If anyone doubts that, they're not saying anything. Deanna knows, but only because I told her. I had to talk to someone. She won't say anything.

Now, the trouble. Barb's parents came round and saw mine, so I had to face a whole lot of questions about you and me. Mum and Dad believed me, thank goodness, when I told them the truth — that you'd kissed me twice and I'd kissed you once — but they looked long and hard at me, I can tell you. Dad commented about how you wrote me an awful lot of letters for just being friends. I never show them your letters, just read them bits out, so that probably made him suspicious. I offered to let him read them, but I was relieved when he said he wouldn't, because I might have had some explaining to do — all those "darlings" you've been throwing in lately, Stephen!

I know Barb's dad went up to the base and saw the Commanding Officer, so they're going to track Roger down, though what good that will do, I don't really know. It makes me so mad. What a horrible way to treat Barb! I'm so glad you're not like him, Stephen, even though — I'm going to blush again — there's part of me that wishes we were together now, because perhaps we would be able to show each other how we feel, instead of always backing away from anything like that. I know I have really grown up in the last year.

Love always,
Ellen

★ ★ ★

1445326 Sgt. S. Dearborn
RAF Lissett
Yorkshire
England

28th of August, 1943

My Darling Ellen,

I am so sorry that you were worried. Reading your letters now, a great, huge bundle of them, I can feel your panic rising when you didn't hear from me for so long. There you were thinking the worst, and I was completely out of it, banged up in the sick bay with pneumonia. You should have written to Dorrie or Mum, they'd have been able to tell you what was up, then you wouldn't have let your imagination run riot.

I don't much remember the last couple of weeks. The medics tell me it was touch and go for a while, and some new wonder drug saved me. You'd laugh, Ellen, to see me now. Skinny isn't in it. I've had to have new holes punched in my belts just to keep my trousers up! Still, one good thing is that I'm being sent home for some convalescent leave. Dorrie's cooking will soon put some meat on my bones for sure. And at least she doesn't burn potatoes! Do you remember that first meal?

I don't like to bother you too much with how I feel and all, and I especially don't like to upset Mum and Dorrie, but I need to tell you about

this. It was a big raid on Hamburg. I don't know
how many planes — we looked like a swarm of
flies. There was heavy flak, just like usual, but we
got through it all right on the way there, dropped
the bombs just like we're told to do. It was an
awful sight, Ellen. It looked like the night had
caught fire. I have to shut it out, tell myself it's
factories and buildings I'm bombing, not people.
I can't think about the people. I don't know.
Maybe I was distracted, maybe it was nothing to
do with me at all, but we took some flak on the
way back. Juddered the whole plane when it hit,
but no one was hurt. The plane still flew, but
everything was sluggish; the controls felt spongy in
my hands. I started praying then, making those
little bargains you do. "If I can get this crate home,
I promise I'll . . ." You know. Our luck held. We
got out over the North Sea closer to England,
thank God, before things really went sour. I didn't
know what do, glide down or tell everyone to bail
out. Oh, we're taught what to do, Ellen, but it's
very different when it's actually happening to you.
I got it down, but I don't know. Everything was
like a dream, like it wasn't really happening to me.

We were shaken up, but we managed to get
the life rafts out before the plane sank. I was the
last one out, jumping for the raft just as it went.
I've probably never told you, but I can't swim,
Ellen. Never learned. If it hadn't been for Paddy
Van Rijnt, my navigator, I'd have gone down with

the plane, that's for sure. It was almost a whole day before we got picked up, one of the longest days of my life, Ellen. We sang, we watched the skies for planes (we've all heard stories about the Germans strafing life rafts), we told each other our life stories — well, a censored version of mine, don't want to scare them, do I? I've never been so happy as when I saw that ship come steaming toward us.

So, here I am, safe and sound. The only bad thing is that the crew got split up while I was ill. I'll have a new one to face when I get back from my leave, but I'm getting a reputation for being a lucky duck, so they'll want to fly with me. Fifteen missions and never a scratch till now. I've always brought my crew safely home.

You had so much news, Ellen, I don't know where to start. I'm glad that you've heard from Barb. She needs a good friend, and I'll always vouch for you in the friendship department. What's it been like working in the office at the gypsum plant? Don't let your dad put too much pressure on you about that. This is just for the summer, right? You're going back to school in the fall (note the Canadianism!), aren't you?

Thank you for the books. I've needed them here. Otherwise I'd have gone bonkers just staring at the sick-bay walls. I was touched that you sent me *The Wind in the Willows*. I'd forgotten that I'd used it to send a message to you. I'm reading the

Walt Whitman you sent. Perhaps in your next letter you can tell me what you think of him, which are your favourite poems? I miss talking to you so much, my love.

All my love,
Stephen

✷   ✷   ✷

Exploding shells rocked the plane. Stephen felt as if they were shaking him loose from reality. Bright flashes of light burst around the perspex canopy, casting odd shadows inside the cockpit. He looked around for the crew. The navigator was turned slightly away. Stephen realized, with growing horror, that he didn't know his name. "Oi," he shouted, relief flooding through him when the navigator acknowledged him. Relief that quickly turned to horror. The man had no face. Underneath his flying helmet was just a featureless blank.

Gagging, Stephen stared at all the switches and dials in front of him. They meant nothing. He looked down at his hands, clumsy in leather gauntlets, clutching the stick. Tentatively, he lifted one, watched how slowly it moved. The air had solidified and it took all his strength to push through it. He pulled hard back. Nothing happened.

Something caused the plane to shake and swerve violently. The smell of smoke was there now. Looking back, Stephen saw flames. A dark figure stood in their midst, holding out his arms as if begging Stephen for something. There was a metallic screaming that hurt Stephen's ears. At first he thought the plane was breaking apart, then he realized that he was making the noise, a high-pitched, keening wail that tore his throat. Through the windscreen of the cockpit, he could no longer see sky, just the gray asphalt of a road that was racing toward him — where no road should be. Instinctively, Stephen threw his hands in front of his face, knowing, even as he did it, that it was useless. Nothing could save him now.

"Stephen!" Dorrie's worried face hung over him. "You were screaming. What's wrong?"

"Nothing." Stephen wanted Dorrie to go. When she didn't move, he shouted, "I told you, it's nothing, just a bad dream. Let me be, for God's sake!" Ignoring the hurt in her eyes, Stephen turned his face to the wall, staring at the familiar blue roses on his wallpaper.

✯　　✯　　✯

200 King Street
Hagersville
Ontario
Canada

27th of October, 1943

My dearest Stephen,
　　Your last letter was so sweet and funny. I like the sound of your new crew, especially the Canadian, Jack Pratchett. He sounds a lot like

Graham, full of himself but nice underneath. I hope you're not serious about growing a moustache to make yourself look older. Three kisses may be your limit if you do.

From what you say, things are heating up. Graham's squadron is doing a lot of missions, too. I often wonder if you fly the same ones. I pray each night that you stay safe. With the time difference, I always imagine that's the time you might be on a raid. I know that you've been added to Mum's prayers, too. She always used to end, "… and keep my boys safe," but now she says, "… keep all the boys safe." It was a really good idea for you to write to her and Dad. I didn't think of doing that, but after that horrible business with Barb and Roger, I think their minds have been put at rest a bit now. Though I think Mum suspects that we're getting a bit serious. She calls you my "young man" sometimes.

My birthday's coming up at the beginning of November. And no, that's not a hint about a present. I was wondering if I could count the ring you gave me as my present, and maybe I'll start wearing it on my finger, rather than hiding it away on a chain around my neck?

It's all set now — I'm leaving school on the Friday after my birthday. I still mind, but there's no point making a fuss. Dad's determined and if I refuse it'll just make life unbearable for everyone. Although I won't be directly doing war work,

I can ease the burden, as so many of their office staff have joined up. So that helps, doesn't it? I'm just like you now, Stephen, putting things on hold for a while, that's all. The only thing that makes it hard is watching Deanna, who hates school, staying on. I can't help envying her, but as soon as her birthday comes round, she's leaving, too. She's got a job in one of the stores, until she's old enough to join the army.

I know you have faith that I'll be a teacher one day; even that funny little sketch you drew of the two of us showed that. Is that really how you see us after the war, with so many papers to mark that the whole room was full of them? Was that room in England or Canada?

I haven't had a letter for three days now. I'm praying that it's just the post that is slow. I can't let myself think of any other reason. I'm going to close now, and if I don't hear from you soon, I'll write to Dorrie.

Your loving,
Ellen

FIFTEEN

A chilly wind blew around Ellen's ankles as she trudged home. It was already dark and the sky so clear a spattering of stars could be seen. Ellen shivered. She wished that she had thought to put her boots on this morning, but she had been too rushed. The new routine of work was proving a challenge, leaving earlier and getting home so much later. Sighing, she wondered again whether she had made a mistake in not staying at the gypsum plant with her father, and instead finding her own job as a clerk in a law office, replacing John Bridie who had been called up for the army. No, she thought, at least this does it on my terms. Ruefully, Ellen smiled, thinking how she had torn up the letter to Stephen about her first day at work, complaining about how tedious it was, and how Miss Penfold the office manager was a miserable old dragon who treated her as if she was a complete dunce. She had felt so much better after writing it, but couldn't send it — her minor miseries seemed trite and foolish.

Turning into her street, Ellen saw that the porch light was on. That meant her mother was home, and a cup of tea would be waiting for her. She smiled in anticipation of curling up in the armchair by the fire, sipping the warm tea and reading any letters that might have come. One from Stephen — that's what Ellen longed for. Although his letters were shorter than ever now, the arrival of one lifted Ellen's spirits, giving her the feeling that everything would work out in the end. Three weeks wasn't the longest time she hadn't had a letter from him — sometimes they arrived in bundles of five or six, despite having been posted at different times. But she always worried, so much so that she had written to Stephen's sister, Dorrie. Her mother had tried to cheer her up by reminding her that they hadn't heard from Graham for nearly a month. Colin had snorted and said, "That's because he hates writing letters and can only be bothered to send an aerogram when you nag him or he wants you to send him something."

Stephen wasn't like that. He wrote every day now, short letters to be sure, in which he sounded tired, even though he was happy to hear from Ellen just once or twice a week.

As the gate clicked open, Colin stood silhouetted in the light from the hallway.

"Ellen, come quick! We've finally got letters from England."

He was waving a bundle of letters, some unopened, which meant that they were addressed to her. For a moment, Ellen felt dizzy as her heart started to race. She ran to Colin, snatched the letters and scanned the envelopes quickly, looking for Stephen's meticulous italics. They were there, but one letter stood out — it had a London postmark, but the writing was unfamiliar. Ellen's fingers felt thick and awkward as she struggled to free the flimsy pages and unfold them. Colin had stayed, watching her. Ellen wanted to shout at him to leave her alone, but the letter screamed at her to be read:

☆　　☆　　☆

79 Gellately Road
New Cross
London
England

5th of November, 1943

Dear Ellen,

    I am sorry to write to you with some very sad news. Stephen's plane was shot down on a bombing raid on the town of Kassel on the night and morning of October 22/23. The Air Ministry have informed us that he was killed when the plane crashed into a road. His crew, with the exception of the tail gunner, parachuted to safety and are now prisoners of war.

    I'm sure you can imagine how sad we are.

Stephen spoke to us a lot about how kind you and your family were to him while he was training. We have just received Stephen's effects, sent by his squadron commander, and there are many letters you wrote to him. He kept them in his locker, apparently, next to his bed. We are glad that Stephen had a such a good friend.

Yours sincerely,
Mrs. D. Anderson (Dorrie)

Ellen stepped blindly past Colin and sank heavily onto the bottom stair. She was dimly aware of Colin shouting, of her mother coming from the kitchen, wiping her hands on her apron and sitting down next to her. She leaned against her mother's side and the tears came — a great, gray wall of tears. Colin knelt in front of her. Gratefully, she put her arms around him, hugging him fiercely against her.

SIXTEEN

79 Gellately Road
New Cross
London
England

22nd December, 1943

Dear Miss Logan,

We thank you for your letter and that of your
family about the loss of our son. Your fondness
for him was obvious in the way you wrote of
him. His death has been a blow; his mother still
has not come to terms with it, and perhaps never
will. Stephen's sister wanted to write, but she
has been a little poorly since the birth of her
daughter. The baby is a little smasher. Dorrie's
decided to call her Stephanie. For my part, I see
now that Stephen felt it was his duty to fight,

and, although I was against his joining up so young, I draw comfort in the fact that he died doing what he believed in.

In this parcel, you will find your letters to Stephen, tied with ribbon, just as they were found in his locker. There was also a book, of poetry I believe, entitled *Sonnets from the Portuguese*, by Elizabeth Barrett Browning. Stephen had written your name on its flyleaf, so we are presuming he wished it sent to you. Another letter was found, one he had written to be opened only after his death. In it, he asked us to keep in touch with you and your family. He also asked that we send to you the contents of his bank account, an amount of just over one hundred pounds sterling, with the instructions that you are to use it to fulfill your dream. That sounds a little cryptic, but I am sure you understand and will follow Stephen's wishes. If you would be so kind as to inform me of the best way to forward this sum to you, I will ensure it is done forthwith.

Yours sincerely,
James Dearborn

☆　　☆　　☆

Sgt. J. Pratchett
Stalag Luft IV
Heydekrug
Germany

22nd of June, 1944

Dear Ellen,

I hope you don't mind me calling you that, because that's how I've always thought of you, that's what Stephen called you. I wrote Stephen's family for your address, because I wanted to tell you how he died.

I don't know whether he ever mentioned me, Jack Pratchett's the name, as he'd only been my skipper for a month or so. I'm Canadian, from Ontario like yourself, although up Sudbury way. Stephen was a damn fine pilot and a great guy. He was quiet, not a gabber like me, but we did talk quite a bit about you and his time with you in Hagersville. From little hints he dropped, I gathered that you were pretty serious and that he was planning on settling in Canada after the war.

The raid on Kassel was a mess. There was an electrical storm that night and going in was like riding a roller coaster because of the flak, but Stephen got us there just dandy. It was coming out we got hit. I knew it was bad right off — there were flames coming out of the tail — Stephen gave us the order to bail out. I was the last one except for him and I yelled, "Get a bloody move on!" but he didn't move. I thought that maybe he had been wounded and I started back in to help him, but he waved me away. I jumped then, messed my ankle up pretty bad on landing. Stephen never made it out. It wasn't till I got my breath back that I realised why. He had steered the plane away from a small village, crashing it into open road. I don't think I would have had the guts to do that.

We were rounded up by some German soldiers pretty soon after and have ended up here.

This is a bit of a nervy, but I was wondering whether you might consider writing to me occasionally. I haven't got a lot in the way of family and, although my mum tries, she's not the greatest letter writer in the world. I remember seeing Stephen laugh when he got your letters. They'd put a smile on his face, which was a good thing.

Yours sincerely,
Jack Pratchett

EPILOGUE

The rain had thinned to a drizzle. Josh Pratchett supposed he should be grateful for that at least. The drive from Hamilton to Toronto had been a nightmare, the rain lashing down making it hard to see, his grandmother sitting unspeaking in the front seat as if she had been carved from ice. He sneaked a glance at her as she strode alongside him down University Avenue. She seemed oblivious to the weather and, indeed, to him. For the life of him, he couldn't figure out why she'd insisted he drive her today. She'd been very mysterious about it, not even telling his father where they were going, other than she needed a ride to Toronto. Josh had been convinced she just wanted to use the time to lecture him about dropping out of university, but the lecture had never come.

"Whoa! Nana, watch out!" Josh shouted. His grandmother had grabbed his arm and pulled him into the road, paying no attention at all to the oncoming cars, and dragging him to an island in the middle of the road where an angular modern sculpture sat. Josh vaguely recognized it, knew that people laughed about it — calling it "Gumby," after the cartoon, but he hadn't the faintest idea in hell what it was there for, or, more to the point, why his grandmother wanted to be there.

"Hold this." The large, loosely wrapped parcel, which had rested on his grandmother's knees on the drive, was now thrust into his arms. "Don't crush it," she admonished Josh, as she fumbled through her bag. Finally, she found what she was searching for — a small, faded jewelry box. Inside, on a tarnished chain, lay a ring unlike any Josh had ever seen. Plain reddish gold, the ring had no fancy stone, just a crest with some letters engraved on it, and two feathery plumes of wings forming the two sides of the shank. His grandmother deftly fastened the chain around her neck, seeming not to care that the ring rested awkwardly on the folds of her scarf.

"Hold on to the end of the bag, Josh, while I pull them out." The "them" were flowers, blue flowers, tied together with a thick, blue ribbon.

"Bachelor's buttons!" Josh blurted out. "But they're summer flowers. Where on earth did you get them, Nana?"

Smiling, his grandmother tapped the side of her nose, as if to warn Josh off from asking questions.

"Cornflowers they're called in England. They always remind me of the color of Air Force uniforms." Her smile grew broader as she indicated the statue. "Quite appropriate, don't you think, for the RCAF memorial?"

So that's what it was! Josh got it. This was some cockeyed tribute his grandmother had dreamed up to Grandpa Jack. The massive heart attack that had killed his grandpa this past spring had been so sudden, so unexpected. Everyone had praised the way that Nana Ellen had coped. She'd even insisted on finishing out the few months left until her retirement from teaching; but Josh remembered his Great-Uncle Stewart warning the family that Ellen always had a tendency to bottle up her feelings.

"This is for Grandpa, right?" Josh looked quizzically at his grandmother. "I don't understand why it had to be today, though. I thought you'd do it on the anniversary of his death, or maybe even Armistice Day next month. Or is this the day that you met?"

His grandmother took a long time answering, and Josh was surprised to see tears in her eyes — tears that she made no attempt to brush away. When she finally spoke, her voice was quiet. "No, Josh. This isn't about your grandpa. Fifty years ago today, October 23rd, 1943, a young Englishman, a pilot, was killed in a bombing raid over Germany. He chose his death willingly, which probably makes him the bravest person I've ever known. He changed my life in so many ways." Absentmindedly, she fingered the ring that hung around her neck. "He was your grandpa's pilot. When he died, he was a little bit younger than you are now." She ignored Josh's in-drawn breath. "I'd very much like to tell you about him. I think you would have liked him. His name was Stephen Dearborn, and the day we first met, he had just very nearly killed my little brother, Colin."

★   ★   ★

AUTHOR'S NOTE

This story is based on fact, albeit facts with which I have taken certain liberties. Canada played a huge role during the Second World War in training allied pilots, some of whom did lie about their age in order to join up. My uncle, Stanley Durrant, was just such a boy; he joined up at sixteen. My character Stephen Dearborn was inspired by him, but not based upon him.

SFTS (Service Flight Training School) 16 was a real place just outside Hagersville, Ontario. The characters in this book are, however, products of my imagination. Sadly, in January of 1942, three trainees were killed when their plane crashed into a farmer's field. This incident suggested to me the event that causes my character to lose his nerve.

The raid on the German city of Kassel took place as described, with 569 allied planes taking part. Forty-three aircraft were lost that night, my uncle's being one of them. Unlike Stephen, he was not flying as a bomber. He had successfully completed one tour of duty, comprising thirty operations, and his crew, rather than having to split up, had volunteered for the very dangerous role of the "Pathfinder," flying in ahead of the bombers to mark the target.

My uncle was wounded on the way back, taking shrapnel in his chest and arm. His navigator gave the order to bail out and dragged my uncle from the plane, pulling the ripcord on his parachute to bring him down safely. Stanley Durrant was nineteen years and three months old. For some time, his family in England did not hear that he was alive. He spent the rest of the war in a German prisoner-of-war camp.

This book was inspired by a comment made by my father, Jimmy Durrant, who served his whole adult life in the RAF. For a writing assignment, I was asking him about his experiences during the fall of France in the summer of 1940. I wanted to know how he felt. He said, "We were just boys, Gill," he said, "just boys."

BIOGRAPHY

Gillian Chan, the popular short-story author of *Glory Days and Other Stories* and *Golden Girl and Other Stories*, was destined to become a writer. Born and raised in the United Kingdom, one of her earliest memories is of being taken in a stroller to the library by her parents. "After being pushed around the adult books, we would head for the "baby" books," she says. "I loved those books. I loved the way they looked, the way they smelled, even the way they tasted!"

Chan's father was a member of the Royal Air Force, which meant the family moved frequently. "A child who moves a lot learns to observe," she says. "I was no exception. I became an observer and retreated into books." For four years after high school, Chan worked at a variety of jobs before entering the University of East Anglia. While a student she met her husband-to-be, Henry. They married in 1982.

Chan taught high school English and drama in Norfolk, eventually ending up as the Head of Resources, "which is a fancy way of saying that, in addition to teaching English, I also ran the school library," she explains. And she wrote stories. "I often couldn't resist doing the assignments I set my students," she remembers. "Sometimes, if I couldn't find a particular story that I wanted, I'd end up writing one for my class."

The Chans fell in love with Canada while on vacation and immigrated to Dundas, Ontario, in 1990. It was during a writing course at McMaster University that Chan's first book was born. Her assignment was to write a short story using an alien first-person voice. "I thought the voice of a 16-year-old boy was as alien as possible," she says. Then she read an article on school bullies and started thinking of all the bullies she'd encountered as a child and as a teacher. The resulting story was "The Buddy System," which led to a related story, "Elly, Nell and Eleanor." After reading Chan's two stories, friends, colleagues and teachers urged her to publish her work.

Chan eventually wrote three more short stories set in a fictional Ontario town called Elmwood, and *Golden Girl and Other Stories* was published by Kids Can Press in 1994. A second collection of Elmwood stories, *Glory Days and Other Stories*, appeared in 1997.

Chan's first novel, *The Carved Box*, is a young adult historical tale, with supernatural undertones, set in 1801 Upper Canada. "It's my homage to Canada," she says.

Chan's love of writing continues unabated, however, her work takes second place to her "very active" six-year-old son, Theo. "I can't wait for the time when he's old enough to read my books," she says.

Golden Girl and Other Stories

Welcome to Elmwood High. Meet Dennis, Elly, Anna, Donna, Bob and Andy. The choices each character faces are never simple; their problems are not easily solved. This collection of hard-hitting short stories delves into the aspirations, thoughts and struggles of high school students everywhere.

★ Junior Library Guild Selection

Glory Days and Other Stories

Welcome back to Elmwood High. Meet Rachel, Art, Rudy, Luisa and Michael. Each one has an important decision to make — and must live with the consequences. Their stories about dating, family, power and identity are filled with strong images, ringing with the emotion and reality of life during the teen years.